Lt. Greg Hammond—He ⬛⬛⬛⬛⬛⬛⬛ he Apaches, but first he had t⬛ ⬛⬛⬛⬛ ⬛⬛⬛⬛ ne warrior.

Chago—Embittered by his father's death at the hands of the white-eyes, he had vowed to regain the Apaches' ancestral lands—with a campaign of terror.

Anita Ballard—She was caught between her love for Greg Hammond and her respect for a father who deserved no respect.

Col. Philip Ballard—Hammond's commanding officer, he admired the young lieutenant—until Hammond discovered his scandalous secret.

Lt. Bill Radcliffe—he had two passions in life: killing Indians—and Anita Ballard.

Simino—He hated all white men, until one of them saved his life. Would he continue to ride with Chago, or would he join his father, a man of peace?

Luanne Marlowe—Determined and ambitious, she knew how to get what she wanted: with her charms if she could, with a gun if she had to.

The Stagecoach Series
Ask your bookseller for the books you have missed

STAGECOACH STATION 43:

APACHE JUNCTION

Hank Mitchum

Created by the producers of
**Wagons West, The Badge,
Abilene,** and **Faraday.**

Book Creations Inc., Canaan, NY · Lyle Kenyon Engel, Founder

BANTAM BOOKS
NEW YORK · TORONTO · LONDON · SYDNEY · AUCKLAND

APACHE JUNCTION
A Bantam Book / published by arrangement with
Book Creations, Inc.
Bantam edition / September 1989

Produced by Book Creations, Inc.
Lyle Kenyon Engel, Founder

ISBN 0-553-28150-X

Published simultaneously in the United States and Canada

Bantam Books are published by Bantam Books, a division of
Bantam Doubleday Dell Publishing Group, Inc. Its trademark,
consisting of the words "Bantam Books" and the portrayal of
a rooster, is Registered in U.S. Patent and Trademark Office
and in other countries. Marca Registrada. Bantam Books,
666 Fifth Avenue, New York, New York 10103.

PRINTED IN THE UNITED STATES OF AMERICA

O   0 9 8 7 6 5 4 3 2 1

STAGECOACH STATION 43:

APACHE JUNCTION

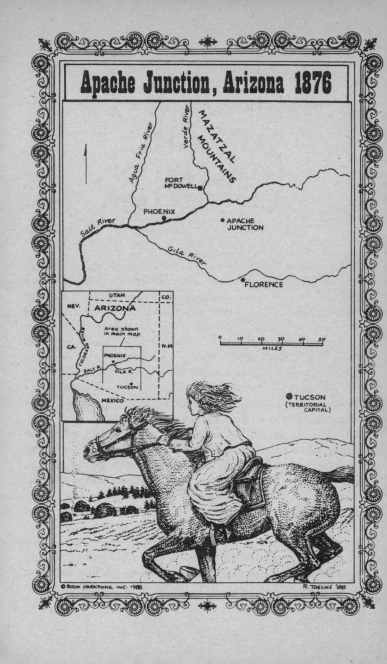

Apache Junction, Arizona 1876

MAZATZAL MOUNTAINS

Agua Fria River

Verde River

FORT McDOWELL

PHOENIX

Salt River

APACHE JUNCTION

Gila River

FLORENCE

UTAH

NEV.

ARIZONA

CO.

Area shown in main map

CA.

COLORADO RIVER

N.M.

PHOENIX

SALT R.

GILA R.

TUCSON

MEXICO

0 10 20 30 40 50
MILES

TUCSON
(TERRITORIAL CAPITAL)

© BOOK CREATIONS, INC. 1988

R. TOELKE '88

Chapter One

Six lathered horses leaned hard into the harness, galloping full speed across the hot Arizona desert, while behind them a Concord coach belonging to the California & Arizona Stage Company bounced along and threw up clouds of sand-colored dust. Over the dry, rugged land gunshots echoed continuously, and puffs of white smoke billowed from the rifles of the whooping Apaches who were in relentless pursuit on sweating pintos. The bounding coach was stuck with dozens of arrows and riddled with bullet holes, and over one side dangled the lifeless body of the shotgunner, two arrows sticking into his chest.

The chase had begun nearly ten miles back when the Indians had suddenly emerged from between two massive rock formations alongside the road, taking the veteran driver by surprise. Led by a young warrior clad in a bright red vest, the Apaches had quickly closed in on the coach, their arrows nocked and ready in their bows. The shotgunner managed to get off one slug before the arrows hissed into his body.

The driver pressed the team into a full gallop, tossing around the six passengers inside the coach like so many dice. They had all boarded in the town of Florence, bound for Apache Junction, thirty miles to the north, and they included three businessmen as well as the wife, son, and daughter of Colonel Philip Ballard, the commandant of Fort McDowell, an army outpost eighteen miles north of their destination. Esther Ballard was shocked by the attack, for nothing like it had happened in more than a year, not since her husband the colonel and Apache chief Amanzus had parleyed and come to terms.

The Apaches had used up all their arrows in the early part of the chase, and now they were blasting away at the bouncing coach with their rifles. The bullets had mortally wounded two of the businessmen, and as the coach drew closer to Apache Junction, the surviving passengers knew that the Indians would try to move in for the kill before it was too late.

Seventeen-year-old Art Ballard glanced at the two dying men slumped on the opposite seat and then at his terrified mother and older sister, Anita, huddled on the floor. Well trained by his father in the use of firearms, the slight, blond young man pulled a revolver from the lifeless hand of one of the men and started firing out the window. His second shot found its mark, knocking an Indian off his pinto, and a look of triumph came over Art's face.

In the seat next to Art, the other male passenger, Spencer Harris, had taken an Apache bullet in his left arm and was fighting to overcome the terrible pain. Nonetheless, he shouted encouragingly, "That's great shooting, son," all the while awkwardly reloading his own revolver to hand to the youth.

Suddenly the stagecoach hit a bump, upsetting one of the bodies and knocking it over on top of Anita Ballard, who screamed. Art turned at the sound, drawing his attention away from the window long enough for an Apache who was coming in close to swing from his horse and get a grip on the stage. Relieved that his sister had not been hit, the youth turned back to the window. Seeing the riderless pinto gallop away, he stuck his head out and spied the Apache working his way toward the front of the coach.

Ballard aimed his revolver at the Indian's belly and fired. The slug bit into the Apache's flesh, and he howled and fell into the dust, his body bouncing and cartwheeling like a rag doll. Taking aim at another Apache, Art squeezed the trigger and heard the hammer come down on an empty cartridge. He pulled his head back inside and quickly exchanged guns with the businessman. The young man was about to fire again when the driver—killed by an Apache bullet—fell from the top of the speeding vehicle past the window and hit the ground.

"They just got the driver!" Art shouted to the others. "I've got to get up to the box and guide the team!" He jerked his head around and asked the businessman, "Mr. Harris, can you fire a gun?"

"I'm left-handed, son," responded Harris, struggling to reload the gun just handed him, "but I'll try!"

Esther Ballard, her long, gray-streaked auburn hair a tangled mass around her face, grabbed her son's arm, tugging hard, trying to get him to remain inside the coach. "Art, if you climb out there you'll be an easy target for those savages!"

"I have to, Ma," Art insisted, pulling his arm free and tucking the revolver under his belt. "Our only hope is to get to Apache Junction! The horses could veer off the road at any second, so someone has to guide them—and there's nobody to do it but me!"

As he spoke the youth snapped open the door and climbed out, grasping the door frame. A bullet chewed wood within inches of his head, but he finally got hold of the luggage rack on top. Another Apache bullet hummed past his ear just as Spencer Harris began shooting. Harris's covering fire gave Art the time he needed to reach the box and climb onto the seat. Seizing the reins, he tightened them just enough to let the horses know they had a driver, and then he let them run.

Harris's revolver ran out of ammunition just as the red-vested Apache leader pulled in close to the stagecoach. Holding his rifle in one hand like a pistol, the Indian fired point-blank at the businessman's head, hitting him between the eyes.

The two women were sprayed with Harris's blood. Anita shrieked; then recovering somewhat, she impatiently brushed her disheveled auburn hair back and, using her sleeve, wiped the blood from her face. Esther, however, was frozen with fear. The younger woman picked up the gun Harris had been using and loaded it, her movements clumsy and uncertain. She crawled to the window and began shooting, but her lack of skill, her desperation, and the jouncing of the coach combined to prevent any of her shots from hitting their targets. Through the churning dust, the young woman watched the red-vested Apache drawing near once again. It was evident from the smirk on his face that he knew he and his men now had the upper hand—and they were ready to close in for the kill.

Lieutenant Greg Hammond led his mounted squad of fourteen men toward Apache Junction, skirting the southern tip of the Mazatzal Mountains. Despite the sweat soaking through his heavy blue wool uniform, the twenty-seven-year-old Hammond cut a dashing figure astride his bay gelding. He was ruggedly handsome, with well-trimmed, curly dark-brown hair and mustache, and he held his tall, muscular body ramrod straight in the saddle. Barely two years out of West Point, he had earned the silver bar of a first lieutenant ten months earlier and was the senior officer of that grade at Fort McDowell.

Hammond had been out on patrol from the fort since sunrise, and now he checked the position of the hot afternoon sun. Then he took out his watch to confirm his estimate that it was nearly two o'clock. As he lifted his hat to wipe his brow with a damp handkerchief, his face reflected the impatience he was feeling.

"Say, Lieutenant, you seem mighty anxious to make sure we're on time," one of his men commented, a wry grin on his face.

Hammond twisted around in the saddle and gave the trooper a sheepish smile. "Yes," he agreed, "as a matter of fact, I am."

"Well, it really wouldn't matter none if we got to Apache Junction a couple of minutes late, now would it?" another trooper asked. "Surely the lovely Miss Ballard won't mind your not bein' there just as the stage pulls in."

Hammond looked sharply at the man. "Well, perhaps Miss Ballard wouldn't mind—but I would. The truth is, I want to be there waiting when Colonel Ballard's family arrives back from their trip."

The first man laughed. "I guess that's what you call being so much in love that even missing a few minutes of time with your heart's delight causes you grief, eh?"

"Yeah," added a corporal, "you're so much in love with Anita Ballard you can hardly stand to be out of her presence."

Hammond tried to frown as if in disapproval of the men's forwardness, but then gave it up and laughed along with them. "Well, I *am* eager to see her again, that's for sure," he admitted. "After all, I've had to stand being out of her presence, as you put it, Kelly, for three months now." He sighed. "This trip that she and her family took to visit their relatives in New Orleans has seemed interminable."

"The question is, Lieutenant," spoke up another, "will Miss Anita be just as eager to see you?"

Hammond looked over his shoulder and leveled his brown eyes on the soldier. "Why don't you admit it, Foley? You're just envious because the beautiful Anita Ballard has chosen me."

The men chuckled at this good-natured riposte; then all fell quiet once again as they made their way through the broiling heat. Only the pounding of horses' hooves, the squeak of saddle leather, and the metallic clanking of military gear broke the silence. From time to time a horse snorted, breaking the monotony of the other steady sounds.

Riding next to Hammond was Lieutenant Bill Radcliffe, who had arrived at Fort McDowell just three days previously. A year younger than Hammond and only recently promoted to first lieutenant, the stocky Radcliffe had a thick mop of curly hair, and his flushed, freckled face seemed to telegraph his easily ignited temper.

Radcliffe pulled out a bandanna and wiped the sweat from his face and the back of his neck. He looked up at the sun and swore, saying, "It's only mid-April, Hammond. What's it gonna be like come July?"

"Hot," came Greg Hammond's terse reply.

"What do you call this?" breathed Radcliffe.

"Warm."

Radcliffe swore again.

Hammond chuckled. "If I understand correctly, you requested duty in Arizona, didn't you?"

"Yes," admitted Radcliffe with a nod, stuffing the bandanna back in his pocket. "I sure didn't think it would be this hot, though."

"Well, at least it's dry—which is far better than that soggy air you had in Virginia."

The two officers could not have been more different in background or attitude. Radcliffe had spent four years at the Virginia Military Institute, and when he had graduated, less than a year ago, his keenest desire was to see action fighting Indians. He had pored over books and periodicals about life in the West and become obsessed with the notion of fighting red-skinned savages. He had read that the Apache were the greatest of warriors among the American Indians, and he had volunteered for duty in the West, specifically requesting Arizona.

Lieutenant Greg Hammond had been born and reared in central New Mexico Territory. He knew the desert and admired everything about it, from its curious and exotic flora and myriad fauna to the Indians who inhabited the harsh yet beautiful terrain. He respected the Apache for their fighting prowess and their desire to live in their ancestral homeland as they had for untold centuries. Unfortunately, the white men had invaded it, and Hammond recognized that the Apache saw them as intruders on their property, reacting no differently from the way the U.S. government would if a horde of foreign invaders were to overrun the country. His reason for requesting duty in Arizona was simple: to keep the peace.

Bill Radcliffe rode silently for several minutes and then asked Hammond, "How long's it been since you killed an Apache?"

"Three months."

Radcliffe reached down, took his canteen from the side of the McLellan saddle, and uncorked it. He took a long pull and then remarked, "That's a long time without any action. Aren't you bored?"

"Nope. I like things quiet," replied Hammond. "As a matter of fact, it's been a good long time since we've had any fighting in this area; the few battles we've fought have been either south or east of here. Last March, Colonel Ballard had a three-day meeting with Chief Amanzus of the White Mountain Apache—they're the most prominent tribe around here—and they came to an agreement. As long as the whites don't make any aggressive moves toward the Apache, the Apache won't bother us."

"So why is the army still here?"

"Well, for one thing, Apaches from other tribes often come through here and make trouble—especially the Jicarillas, Chiricahuas, and Mescaleros—and we have to be here to handle them. And for another thing, this treaty is only good as long as Amanzus is in charge of the White Mountain tribe. If he loses power or dies, we could be at war again. With more and more white people moving here from the East, we have to be on hand to protect them."

"Good," Radcliffe declared, grinning. "I'll be glad to

do my part. The more Apaches I kill, the safer it'll be around here for everybody."

Lieutenant Greg Hammond gave the officer a stern look but said nothing.

Radcliffe spoke again. "Lieutenant, this daughter of the colonel's. I've heard the men talk about her."

"Oh?"

"Yeah. They say she's quite a feast for the eyes."

A softness came over Greg Hammond's face. "Yes, she's the kind of woman men dream about," he mused, giving Radcliffe a sidelong glance. "She's small and slender with eyes as blue as the sky, skin like the petal of a pink rose, hair that reminds me of a flaming sunset, and . . . a face so beautiful that words almost fail me. She—"

"You engaged to her?" interrupted Radcliffe.

"No. That is, not yet. But that's going to happen pretty soon."

Radcliffe stared at his fellow officer. "You sound awfully confident. Haven't some of the other men tried to give you some competition?"

"A little," admitted Hammond, "but nothing serious. It's very clear to everyone that Anita has eyes only for me."

Lieutenant Bill Radcliffe settled into his saddle. "I see," was all he said.

It was just past two o'clock when Greg Hammond led his squad into Apache Junction and hauled up in front of the stage-line office. Sitting in front was an army wagon from Fort McDowell, and six horses with U.S. Army brands on their rumps stood tethered to the hitch rail, lazily swatting flies with their tails. Hammond looked across the street and saw seven troopers sitting on the ground under a huge, leafy oak tree that grew between two clapboard buildings.

The men in the shade called out greetings to their comrades as a husky sergeant rose to his feet and hurried toward Greg Hammond.

"Afternoon, Lieutenant," the sergeant declared with a snappy salute.

Saluting back, Hammond dismounted. "I assume the stagecoach hasn't arrived yet, Sergeant O'Malley," he commented.

"No, sir," the sergeant confirmed. Then, with a twinkle in his eye, he added, "And I assume it just so happened that your route of patrol brought you into Apache Junction at the same time the stagecoach is due."

Hammond grinned wryly. "Coincidence, Sergeant O'Malley, mere coincidence. But I figured as long as we were so close by, we might just as well assist in escorting the colonel's family back to the fort."

"Whatever you say, Lieutenant," chuckled O'Malley.

Hammond turned to his men and told them, "You fellas can dismount and sit in the shade with the others. I'll join you in a moment." He strode to the stage-line office and stepped inside. A quick glance at the clock on the wall told him that it was eight minutes past two.

The agent, Wally Becker, a small man in his late forties, looked up from his desk and said, "Hello, Lieutenant. Looks like you've got half of Fort McDowell out there. Someone important coming in on the stage?"

"Yes," replied Hammond, lifting his hat and wiping his sweating brow, "Colonel Ballard's wife, son, and daughter. The stage is running somewhat late, I gather."

"Yep, a bit," Becker confirmed. "Agent down in Florence wired to say it was about a half hour late in leaving this morning. They had to wait for passengers connecting from the Southern Pacific Mail Line, which had a coach coming in from the east. We try to work things out so folks can make the changeover with no trouble." He pointed to the chalkboard across the room. "There's the new arrival time."

Hammond followed the direction of the agent's finger, reading the information: *California & Arizona Stage Company: April 16, 1876. Florence stage will arrive 2:30 p.m.* Looking back at the agent, the young lieutenant touched his hat brim. "Much obliged," he said. "The Ballards were supposed to be aboard the Southern Pacific coach, so I'm glad your men waited for it." He turned and stepped outside.

As he crossed the street toward his men lounging in the shade, Hammond instinctively looked southward. There was no sign of the vehicle that was carrying the woman he loved. The troopers started to get up as he drew nearer, but the officer waved his hand and told them, "Relax, fellas. Stay comfortable." He himself, though, remained standing, never taking his gaze from the direction from which the stage would be arriving.

Sergeant Francis O'Malley laughed. "Just can't wait to see her, eh, Lieutenant?"

Hammond turned his head and grinned at him. "You've got that right, O'Malley."

"What's takin' you so long to ask the colonel for her hand, anyway, Lieutenant?" O'Malley asked with an easy familiarity. "Legs a little shaky?"

Hammond removed his hat, wiped his brow yet again, and replied, "I will admit I'm a bit nervous about broaching the subject to the colonel. I guess any man who asks a father for his daughter's hand is rather on edge when it comes right down to it—and in this case, there's even more to make a guy nervous, since Anita's father is my commanding officer."

"That would tend to water a man's knees some," admitted the trooper.

Dropping his hat back on his head, Hammond continued, "Timing's an important factor in matters such as this, too. A man wants to work it just right, so that—"

The lieutenant's remarks were cut short by the sudden appearance of a rider galloping in from the south and shouting excitedly, although from that distance the words were indistinct. The rider apparently spotted Hammond, for he raced his horse in his direction, skidding to a halt just in front of him. Sliding from the saddle, the man gasped, "Lieutenant, am I glad to see you! The stagecoach is comin' toward town full speed, bein' chased by Apaches!"

Greg Hammond immediately ordered his men to mount up. Even before all the troopers could dash to their horses and bound into their saddles, the lieutenant was astride his own horse and charging down Main Street, shouting, "Let's go!"

Sergeant Francis O'Malley, who had driven the wagon from Fort McDowell and therefore had no horse to mount, spotted a gray and white piebald tied to a nearby hitch rail. With no thought to the consequences of conscripting the animal, he ran to it and leaped into the saddle, galloping out of town slightly behind the others.

Art Ballard sat atop the stagecoach, driving and shooting at the same time. Just as the red-vested Apache took aim to fire at him, one of the other braves shouted and pointed, "Chago! Soldier-coats!"

The Apache leader whipped his head around and stared into the distance. Coming toward the stagecoach at full gallop was a troop of blue-uniformed riders, and at the sight of them Chago pulled up and signaled for his men to turn back. The six men obeyed, jerking their pintos to a halt and pivoting them around to race in the opposite direction.

Young Ballard spotted the soldiers, too, and with relief washing over him like a cool shower, he pulled the panting, foam-flecked team of horses to a halt. Jamming the revolver under his belt, he raised a hand and waved at the rescuers, whooping loudly himself.

His sister stuck her head out the window, and Art shouted, "We're saved! Look!" Blinking against her tears, Anita smiled joyfully as the soldiers came toward the stage in a cloud of dust.

Hammond and his men rumbled to a stop, their faces

reflecting their anger as they assessed the arrow- and bullet-riddled stagecoach.

"Are you fellas ever a sight for sore eyes!" gasped Art as he began to descend from the box.

Greg Hammond leaped from his saddle and yanked open the door. Anita literally fell into his arms, bursting into tears and sobbing his name. His worried eyes took in the blood on her dress, and he held her at arm's length, asking, "Darling, are you all right?"

Anita shuddered, explaining that it was blood from one of the dead men inside the coach. She broke into tears again and pressed her head against Hammond's chest, clinging tightly to him. When he had ascertained that no harm had come to Esther Ballard either, Greg Hammond sighed, and said, "Thank God none of you was harmed." Then he commanded, "Sergeant O'Malley, you and your men hoist the bodies onto the top of the coach. Assign one man to accompany the stage; he can return the horse you commandeered while you take his." Turning to Art, he said, "Son, I want you to drive the coach into town, stop at the undertaker's with those poor passengers and crew, and then go to the stage-line office and wait there until my men and I return."

"Return?" the youth asked. "Where are you going?"

"After the Apaches," Greg Hammond growled. "They're going to answer for this."

Chapter Two

For five years hatred of the white men had been smoldering inside young Chago like a dormant volcano; now it had finally erupted, spewing out revenge and cruelty. It was back then that his father, Chief Pakima, had engaged his warriors in a bloody battle with soldiers from Fort McDowell. But the white men had triumphed and captured Pakima, and then horribly tortured him. Chago fled the central Arizona area shortly after his father's death, going north to help his brothers, the Jicarilla Apaches. Having lost their fighting leader during a fierce battle with the army in the northern Arizona mountains, the Jicarillas reluctantly put Chago in charge—and discovered that the supremely intelligent young man was a ferocious and indomitable fighting machine.

Despite Chago's efforts, though, the Jicarillas succumbed over time to the more modern and powerful military weapons of the white man's army. They became subdued and peaceable, and there was no more fighting to be done. Chago left the tribe in the hands of a new chief, Ramino, and returned to his White Mountain people.

After his return he was plagued anew by nightmarish memories of his father's horrendous death—and he vowed to rid his ancestral home of all whites. Finding warriors among the White Mountain Apaches to join him was easy, and they laid plans to make systematic attacks on stagecoaches, wagon trains, and other travelers, with the intent of killing every white person they encountered. Today's attack on the Apache Junction stage was just the first of many to come.

Now the young warrior seethed as he and his six men raced back down the road to pick up their three dead comrades, whose bodies were scattered over a three-mile stretch. He reviled the soldiers for showing up when they did, for their appearance had prevented him from finishing off the last of the travelers.

When he reached the first slain warrior, Chago slid from his pinto's back and stood over the lifeless form, staring at the gaping bullet hole in the corpse's belly. One of the other braves hurried after the dead man's horse, which had strayed to the shade of a huge rock a hundred yards away; the other five men eyed their leader as he stood in the middle of the road as unmoving as a tree, his swarthy face twisted with hatred as he cursed the white men.

Chago was an ugly man, made even uglier by his rage. His wide-set black eyes sat above a crooked nose that had been broken several times. Prominent cheekbones framed a thin, cruel-looking mouth that turned down even when he smiled, which was seldom. His hair, black like his eyes, hung to his shoulders and was held in place by a red bandanna that he wore around his head as a sweatband. The young warrior had never been seen without the red vest on his otherwise naked upper body since the day he had taken it off a gambler when the Apaches had attacked a stagecoach several weeks earlier. And he was seldom seen without his knife, strapped around his waist in a leather sheath, or the Remington .44 seven-shot repeater stolen from a dead soldier during a battle in the northern mountains.

As the brave who had gone to retrieve the stray pinto was drawing near, leading it behind him as he rode his own horse, one of the others pointed northward and shouted, "Chago! The soldier-coats!"

Chago cursed again; then his face twisted bitterly and he declared, "The white devils outnumber us. We will have to come back for our dead later."

Fleeing, the Apaches rode by the other two Indian bodies lying on the dusty ground. Then Chago veered his horse off the road and headed into the barren hills as the dust cloud being raised by the approaching soldiers grew ever larger.

Passing the bodies of the three Apaches, Lieutenant Greg Hammond and his men also left the road, giving chase in a thundering gallop. Hammond shouted, "Fan out! They'll reach the hills before we do and take their stand, but we outnumber them more than two to one! Let's hit them from three sides!"

While his men obeyed Hammond's command, Lieutenant Bill Radcliffe stayed at his fellow officer's side as he had been instructed to do in case of a confrontation. He had never seen action before, and there was a wild look in his eyes as he anticipated it.

The fleeing Apaches suddenly disappeared behind large rocks imbedded in the sandy bluffs. Seconds later, puffs of white smoke lifted into the clear air as rifles barked and bullets whined. Before the soldiers could react, one of them took a slug in the chest and fell from his mount.

The death of their comrade spurred the men in blue to leap off their horses and belly down on the ground, crawling and shooting from three directions. Most of the Indians had single-shot rifles, while all the troopers had repeaters. The hail of hot lead biting into the rock, breaking off fragments, made it difficult for the Apaches to rise up and shoot. However, Chago exhorted them, and they incautiously poked their heads out and returned fire.

As the din of the battle rose to a crescendo, another trooper fell dead. The two lieutenants crawled straight in, firing their revolvers from prone positions. Bill Radcliffe was grinning fiendishly, snapping off his shots rapidly, but Greg Hammond was more circumspect, firing only when he could actually see an Indian.

Soon Radcliffe's hammer clicked on an empty chamber. Swearing, he reached for the leather packet on his belt for more cartridges—but at the same time, an Apache rose from behind a boulder and took dead aim at his head. When the young lieutenant looked up to see the muzzle trained on him, his face blanched, his body froze, and he waited for the bullet to hit him. But Greg Hammond, seeing Radcliffe's predicament, swerved the gun in his hand, aimed at the Apache, and quickly squeezed off a shot. The slug ripped into the Indian's chest before he could fire at Radcliffe, and he dropped his rifle, standing straight up as he clutched at the wound. Then he pitched headlong over the top of the rock to the ground below.

The soldiers crawled closer to the rocks from all three sides, and above the thunder of the guns Chago's voice could be heard commanding his men to draw back. His red vest was a bright flash on the dun-colored landscape as he darted between two huge boulders, heading toward the hills behind him.

Hammond rose up on one knee and shouted for his men to close in. Bill Radcliffe was still reloading as Hammond started running toward the rocks. The older lieutenant abruptly halted in his tracks and looked over his shoulder, ordering, "Come on, Radcliffe!"

Gritting his teeth, Radcliffe growled, "I've got to get this gun loaded!"

"You wasted your ammunition," Hammond scolded him. "You shouldn't fire until you have a target!"

Radcliffe's face flushed an angry red. He disliked being reprimanded by a fellow officer, even one who had just saved his life. "Don't tell me my job, Hammond!"

"I won't when I see you doing it right," countered the lieutenant. "Now come on!"

Snapping his gun shut, Radcliffe followed Hammond and the other men up into the rocks. The soldiers climbed past the bodies of three Indians, which meant that there could only be four Apaches left, including the leader in the red vest. Suddenly Chago and his men appeared from behind the rocks, and the Apaches fired a quick volley of shots, taking down two more troopers. The soldiers returned the fire, and half a dozen slugs hit the rock where the Indians had been, but they had vanished like ghosts.

"Go after them, men!" shouted Hammond.

The soldiers let loose a battle cry as they scrambled over and around the rocks. Four of the blue-coated men discovered three Apaches reloading their single-shot rifles and pumped them full of bullets. As the echo of their blazing guns faded, they could hear a horse galloping off. A beefy sergeant clambered up the highest rock and swore when he reached the top. Looking down at Hammond, he pointed toward the north, shouting, "The vermin in the red vest is gettin' away, Lieutenant!"

Greg Hammond raced up to join his sergeant and followed the man's finger, watching as the Apache leader rode farther and farther away.

"You gonna go after him, Lieutenant?" the sergeant asked.

Hammond shook his head. "No sense in trying, Sergeant Foster. He's got a sizable lead already. By the time I got back to my horse, he'd have vanished into the hills."

Suddenly, Bill Radcliffe raced down the slope, heading for his horse. "If you won't go after that filthy redskin," he yelled over his shoulder at Hammond, "I will! Seems to me that someone has to uphold the standards of the United States Army."

Watching the younger lieutenant with disgust, Greg Hammond shouted, "Get back here, Lieutenant! We don't have time for empty heroics!"

But his words were ignored. Technically, Hammond knew he could order the hot-headed younger man to obey his command, for although both men held equal rank, Greg Hammond, as senior officer, was in command. But out here on the frontier the rule books and military codes were frequently bent, and after wavering a few seconds, Hammond finally decided to let Radcliffe get his feet wet in the field. Sighing, the officer turned to Sergeant Foster and two other troopers and ordered, "You men had better follow the lieutenant. No telling what kind of trouble he'll get into by himself. There may well be more Apaches hiding out there somewhere, and he could ride himself right into a trap."

"Yes, sir!" the three troopers said in unison, snapping off salutes before dashing to their mounts.

Pushing his hat back on his head, Hammond muttered to himself, "I hope he learns soon that maneuvers on the frontier aren't necessarily done the way they're described in the books he read back at V.M.I."

He watched the sergeant and his two men ride off. Then, turning to the remaining troopers, he ordered, "We've got four dead men. Let's load their bodies on their horses while we wait for Lieutenant Radcliffe and the others to return."

Bill Radcliffe lashed his horse, bent on catching the bloodthirsty Apache, who was now a half mile ahead of him, his long black hair flying in the wind as he raced across the rolling desert. Both riders skillfully avoided the huge clumps of prickly pear cactus, mesquite bushes, and towering saguaros. Suddenly the Indian whirled his pinto back around and charged toward the oncoming soldier, his rifle leveled.

At that same instant Radcliffe felt the world turn upside down around him. His horse had stepped in a prairie dog hole, throwing him from the saddle. Radcliffe hit the ground, rolling in the dirt. The impact of the fall dazed him, knocking the wind from his lungs.

Shrieking in agony, the horse lay with its belly on the ground and its right foreleg buried in the hole. Radcliffe rose to his feet, staggering like a drunk as he gasped for breath.

Two hundred yards away the Apache waved his rifle in a show of triumph as he guided his pinto straight for the army officer. It seemed as if he had decided first to run the soldier down with his galloping horse and then kill him with a bullet.

Radcliffe shook his head, trying to clear it. Blinking at the oncoming rider, he pulled out his revolver, cocked it, and waited for the Indian to get closer. But the red man abruptly jerked back the reins and halted his animal in a cloud of dust. At the same time, Radcliffe heard the pounding of hooves behind him, and he whipped his head around to see three soldiers coming at a full gallop. Looking back toward Chago, he barely caught a glimpse of the warrior as he disappeared over a sandy rise.

The three troopers thundered in, and the sergeant looked at the horse and then asked, "Are you all right, Lieutenant?"

"Yes," Bill Radcliffe grunted, sucking in a deep breath. Turning to the suffering horse, he aimed his revolver at its head and fired. The shot echoed over the desert floor and the animal slumped down, dead. Thanking the men for coming to his aid, the lieutenant swung up behind one of the troopers, and they quickly returned to the others.

The squad started back toward Apache Junction with their dead, one of whose horses Bill Radcliffe now rode. Coming upon the second Indian who had been left behind by his fleeing tribesmen, the soldiers were startled to discover that he was not lying where he had been when they had passed him the first time. Rather, he was alive and had managed to crawl to the side of the road into the shade of a large boulder.

Hammond, riding in the lead with Radcliffe beside

him, raised a hand to halt the small column of men. He dismounted and cautiously approached the wounded Apache, who was clutching a bleeding right shoulder and eyeing the soldiers warily. The lieutenant leaned over and pulled the Indian's knife from its sheath, tossing it away. Radcliffe then dismounted, and the rest of the men followed suit.

Bill Radcliffe came up beside Hammond and stood looking down at the fallen Apache, hostility evident in his amber-colored eyes. "So we got one still breathing, huh?" he hissed.

Ignoring Radcliffe, Hammond knelt beside the seriously wounded Apache and asked, "Did the bullet go through your shoulder, or is it still in there?"

The Apache's face was stoical as he answered in halting English, "It pass through."

Looking up at his fellow officer, Hammond told him, "Radcliffe, there's a bandage roll and some alcohol in my saddlebags. Get them for me."

Radcliffe stared at Hammond incredulously. "What are you doing?" he gasped. "You're not gonna bandage him up?"

"This isn't a question-and-answer session, Lieutenant. The man is bleeding badly, and I gave you a direct order to get the medical supplies out of my saddlebags."

Radcliffe stiffened. "I'm not helping a man who is my enemy. If you do, you'll have to get them yourself."

Hammond's eyes flashed, but before he could pull rank, Sergeant Foster intervened. "I'll get them, Lieutenant."

Under Bill Radcliffe's hot glare, Hammond called to one of the other men to bring a canteen. The trooper obeyed immediately and hurried to the lieutenant's side, placing the canteen in Hammond's hand. He brought it to the Indian's lips, tilting it slowly and letting him take the water in small sips.

Although his face still showed no expression, there was gratitude in the Apache's black eyes. Hammond asked, "What's your name?"

"Simino."

"Well, Simino," remarked Hammond, "when we rode by here a little while ago, I'd have sworn you were dead."

"When bullet struck me," replied the Apache, "it knocked me from my horse onto my head. I stay unconscious until short while ago."

Sergeant Foster thrust the bandage roll and a small bottle of alcohol into Greg Hammond's hands. "Here you go, Lieutenant," he said softly, at the same time eyeing Bill Radcliffe.

Radcliffe suddenly blurted, "Hammond, this filthy scum is your enemy! Have you forgotten that he attacked the stagecoach with your woman on it? He'd have killed her if he could!"

"I'm fully aware of what he did and what his intentions were," snapped Hammond. "You're right, he is my enemy. But for now he's my *wounded* enemy, which throws a different light on the picture."

Radcliffe's fury mounted. "What difference does it make that he's wounded? He's still your enemy! I've read about the cruelties and atrocities of these vicious people. They're wild savages! Do you know what he'd do to you if you were in his place? He'd torture you and then kill you, that's what he'd do!"

Hammond stood up and stared intently at Radcliffe. "Is that what you want us to do, Lieutenant?" he asked in a steely voice. "Torture him and then kill him?"

"Sure. Why not give him a little of his own medicine?" the younger lieutenant growled.

Shaking his head, Hammond retorted, "Radcliffe, we would be no different than they if we behaved in the same manner. Torture is torture . . . no matter who's doing it." Pointedly ignoring the contemptuous expression on Radcliffe's face, he knelt down again and finished ministering to the Indian. As he knotted the end of the bandage that he had wrapped around Simino's shoulder, he told the Apache, "That'll do until we get you to the fort."

Radcliffe's wrath exploded again. "Hammond," he blared, whipping out his revolver, "don't tell me the army will provide treatment for this savage! I won't stand for it! This vermin needs to die right now!"

The troopers all tensed as Greg Hammond leaped to his feet, standing between Radcliffe and the Indian. Hammond's stony face was immobile, and a heavy silence grew between the two officers. Finally Hammond ordered, "Put the gun away, Lieutenant Radcliffe."

Defiance was written all over Radcliffe's face as he coolly retorted, "You may have seniority, Lieutenant Hammond, but I'm sure I don't have to remind you that I was sent to Arizona by the United States government for the purpose of controlling and if necessary killing hostiles— one of whom is lying at my feet. They have been allowed far too much freedom as it is, resulting in their treating whites as they do—and I'm going to do my part to retaliate. You may believe in pampering them, Lieutenant, but I believe in killing them. I'm not soft like you! As the man said, the only good Indian is a dead Indian—and I'm going to turn this Apache scum into a good one right now!"

Greg Hammond stared at the younger officer for a long moment. "I won't make an issue of my seniority, Lieutenant Radcliffe, because I believe that officers should set an example to their men as to how they should conduct themselves." Hammond spoke coldly, enunciating each word precisely for effect. "But let me get something planted straight in your mind right now: Soldiers of the United States Army do not make war on wounded men. Simino will be taken to the fort as a prisoner and will be given medical treatment by the post physician. I'll consider that your judgment has been temporarily impaired by irrational hatred as well as inexperience, so I'll let this pass. Just let me remind you that our captive is a human being, and your duty is to treat him as such."

Radcliffe's jaw muscles worked as the man gritted his teeth. "I told you, Lieutanant Hammond, that I requested assignment out here to kill Apaches. And that's exactly what I plan to do."

"That's fine when it's on the field of battle," replied Hammond. "But when the enemy is wounded and no longer a threat, we do not murder him."

"Murder!" gasped Radcliffe. "How can you call it murder? As soon as this animal is healed, he'll try to kill us!"

"That may well be, Lieutenant, but right now Simino is wounded, and he is our prisoner. We will take our prisoner to the fort and Doc Wheatley will patch him up."

Bill Radcliffe sneered, "Seems to me you're fighting for the wrong side, Hammond!" Then, without warning, he aimed the revolver at the Apache, snapping back the hammer. "I know how to handle savages!" he bellowed.

Instantly Greg Hammond's foot lashed out and kicked the gun from Radcliffe's hand. The weapon fired harmlessly into the air as it sailed several feet away and landed in the dirt. Furious, Radcliffe swore and swung a wild punch at Hammond's jaw, but the lieutenant saw it coming and dodged, and then unleashed a ferocious punch of his own. It connected solidly, and Radcliffe landed flat on his back with Hammond standing over him, poised to strike again if he had to.

"Lucky for you, Radcliffe, that I'm more than willing to settle our differences man-to-man and ignore the fact that I'm the commanding officer—because if I didn't choose to overlook it, I could haul you up on charges of insubordination and striking a ranking officer so fast it'd make your head spin!"

Gaining his feet, Radcliffe growled, "You're gonna be sorry you made that decision, Hammond!" He suddenly charged, fists flying, but Hammond ducked the first blow and blocked the second, and then managed to chop the lieutenant smartly on the ear. Radcliffe staggered slightly, but rebounded with a punch of his own, landing a blow squarely on Hammond's chin.

The men continued to trade punches, egged on by the troopers standing around and enjoying the spectacle of two officers fighting. All of them knew that Radcliffe could be in deep trouble for insubordination, but Hammond was the sort of man who would settle matters here and now, not by the army rule book.

Both fighters' faces were bloodied, although Radcliffe seemed to have gotten the worst of the battle. Finally Hammond landed an uppercut that bested his opponent. Radcliffe went down and lay in the dust, panting for breath.

Sucking hard for air himself, Greg Hammond brushed at the blood and dirt on his uniform. One of the men handed him a canteen, and he poured the cool water over his head to clear it both inside and out. Then he took a swig and washed out his bloodied mouth, spitting a stream of red into the dust.

Radcliffe got first to his knees and finally to his feet. He made a slight move toward Hammond, but then apparently thought better of it. Without another word he pivoted sharply and, a sullen look on his battered face, strode to his horse, accompanied by the snickers of the troopers.

After Simino had been placed upon his pinto, the squad mounted up and started for Apache Junction. Although Radcliffe remained silent during most of the journey, his thoughts were clear. Everyone riding with him—especially Greg Hammond—wondered how a man filled with so much hatred could serve the cause of peace.

Chapter Three

As the small column of soldiers rode toward Apache Junction, Lieutenant Hammond positioned himself between Radcliffe and the wounded Apache. Looking across at the Indian, Hammond commented, "I think I've seen you before. You're of the White Mountain tribe, aren't you?"

For a long moment Simino said nothing. He wiped his sweating hand on his blue denim pants—taken a few weeks earlier from a white man—and then adjusted the knee-high goatskin moccasin on his right leg. Finally he nodded and replied woodenly, "Yes."

"Were all of you who attacked the stagecoach today White Mountain?"

"Yes."

"So Chief Amanzus has broken his treaty with our colonel," Hammond muttered.

Simino shook his head emphatically, flapping his long black hair and slightly loosening the red-and-white patterned bandanna tied around his head. "Chief Amanzus did not order the attack," he responded flatly.

"Then who did?"

"Chago. He is great warrior, and he plans many more attacks. He will not die easy. You know of him?"

Greg Hammond rubbed his chin. "Seems I've heard the name somewhere. Who is he?"

"He is son of Chief Pakima."

"Oh, yes," said Hammond, "the one who was captured and tortured to death by some soldiers from the fort. Colonel Ballard told me about him. Yes, now I remember. That's when I heard this Chago's name. The colonel told me about him and his need for vengeance against white men for killing his father." Hammond shifted in the saddle and looked directly at Simino. "So this trouble is being caused by Chago, eh? Tell me, why has Chago waited all this time? After all, his father was killed some years ago."

Simino explained how Chago had gone north to fight with a brother tribe and had only recently returned, determined to launch an all-out offensive against whites and to wipe out all white travelers.

Nodding thoughtfully, the lieutenant said, "I see. So what we have to look forward to is a string of bloodthirsty killings?"

"Yes."

"Are they to be carried out with Chief Amanzus's blessing?"

Simino looked away from the soldier's piercing gaze. "I . . . I would not say with his blessing, Lieutenant."

"But he knows about them and will do nothing to stop them?"

"I am not told such things," replied the Apache.

Hammond lifted his dusty hat and wiped away the muddy film from his brow, then asked, "And what about you, Simino? Did you volunteer to do this with Chago?"

"I am twenty-three years in this world. I have seen nothing good come from white man until today, when you stopped that man from killing me." He gazed past Hammond to Radcliffe. Then his hitherto impassive face took on a fiercely proud expression. "I am devoted to my people, to Apache nation. This is land of my fathers, but white man is stealing it from us."

Greg Hammond cast a glance at Radcliffe. These were just the kind of words that would set the younger officer aflame.

"Would you feel different, Lieutenant," continued Simino, "if this land belonged to your fathers and Apache had stolen it?"

Hammond was silent for a moment; then he looked at the Apache and replied, "In all honesty, Simino, I would feel exactly as you do."

Radcliffe spat in disgust. Fixing the Indian with hot eyes, he rasped, "You're a liar, Indian! I've read all about you savages, and I know that no Apache wants peace with white men!" He spat again, adding, "If I had my way, you'd be lying back there on the side of the road with a bullet in your head!"

"That's enough, Radcliffe!" Hammond roared. "You're a member of the United States Army, not some vigilante group. I expect you to act accordingly."

Radcliffe's eyes narrowed as he looked at his fellow officer. "I don't get it, Hammond. You ought to want him dead, too. After all, he was trying to kill Anita Ballard on that stagecoach."

Hammond's face grew dark. "That's true—and if I had been on the stage I'd have done my best to kill him. But the picture has changed now. As I said, the U.S. Army doesn't make war on wounded men."

Simino gave the fiery lieutenant a caustic look but said nothing.

"All right," Hammond shouted to his men, "let's pick up our pace and reach Apache Junction as soon as possible! I want to deliver the Ballards back to Fort McDowell before dark! Move it!"

As the procession continued at a fast trot, Radcliffe held his horse back, falling into place behind Hammond. He rode silently the rest of the way into town, all the while glaring at the back of Hammond's head, his eyes filled with fury.

*   *   *

When Hammond led his men and their wounded prisoner into Apache Junction, they stopped first at the far end of town to leave the bodies of the dead soldiers with the undertaker, who was already dealing with the bodies of the passengers and crew from the stage. Then the squad made its way along Main Street to the California & Arizona office. There the bullet-riddled coach was parked in front—minus its exhausted team, which had been led to the livery stable to be cooled and watered.

People were gathered around the coach, talking and excitedly pointing to the bullet holes, and when the column of riders in blue drew near, all eyes turned in their direction. The sight of the wounded Apache on his pinto created an instant hubbub, and the commotion apparently had been heard inside the office, for suddenly Anita Ballard appeared at the door. The young woman was then joined by Esther and Art Ballard, and the three of them stepped out onto the boardwalk. At the sight of Greg Hammond, Anita dashed into the street, waiting impatiently for him to dismount.

The dust-covered lieutenant slid from his saddle and gathered Anita into his arms. As he comforted her, Radcliffe looked on with envy. It was clear that if he could, he would possess her himself.

"Thank God, you're safe," Anita whispered to the handsome lieutenant. "I was so worried."

He drew back from her slightly and gave her a wry smile. "Nothing to worry about, sweetheart. After all, I've got all the reason in the world to stay alive and healthy— and I'm holding it here in my arms."

Blinking back tears, Anita asked, "Greg, are we going to have more war with the Apaches?"

He sighed. "Could be, honey. I'm not too sure Amanzus is going to stick by his agreement with your father." He released the beautiful young woman. "Speaking of your father, it's high time we get you back home before he sends out more troops looking for us." He turned to his men, ordering, "Put Simino in the wagon, fellas. I don't think he can stay on his horse all the way to the fort."

Looking over her shoulder, the redhead finally noticed the wounded Apache. She focused on his face and gasped. "Oh, good heavens! Greg, that Indian's the one who put a bullet through one of the passenger's heads! Surely you're not going to let him ride with us! He's nothing but a murderer!"

Radcliffe moved closer. "She's absolutely right, Hammond," he declared. "Why, I can't imagine what you're thinking, forcing these good people to ride with that bloodthirsty savage." The smirk on his face spoke volumes as to his intent.

Greg Hammond ignored the inflammatory words, but they obviously had their intended effect, for Anita looked beseechingly into his eyes and asked, "Greg, isn't there some other way you can take the Indian to the fort? I really don't wish to ride in that wagon with him! Who knows what he'll do!"

Hammond put his hand under Anita's delicate chin. "Believe me, if there were another way, I'd use it. But he's badly wounded, and I doubt he'd survive the ride to the fort on his horse. I'm surprised he's made it this far." He gazed into her eyes and told her softly, "Surely you don't believe for a moment that I'd put you or your family in any danger, Anita? I'll have two troopers in the wagon with Simino; he won't be a threat, I assure you. Why—"

"Don't worry, ma'am," Radcliffe broke in. "I wouldn't let anything happen to a beautiful creature like you."

Anita turned and looked directly at the officer for the first time. Blushing slightly, she observed, "I don't believe we've met. I'm Anita Ballard, Colonel Ballard's daughter."

Radcliffe pressed as close to the young woman as social convention would allow. Removing his hat, he told her effusively, "And I'm your devoted servant, Lieutenant William Radcliffe. I am absolutely delighted to make your acquaintance."

Anita blushed again and looked down at her feet.

Lieutenant Hammond put a proprietary arm around the young woman's shoulders and explained tonelessly, "Lieutenant Radcliffe arrived at the fort just a few days ago."

"I see," Anita murmured, giving the younger officer a pleasant smile.

Radcliffe pounced on the opportunity. "The first day I arrived at Fort McDowell, ma'am, I heard several of the men saying the colonel had a beautiful daughter. May I say that their words could not come close to what my eyes tell me at this moment."

Anita looked embarrassed, and Hammond's face flushed with anger. Turning to his troops, he called out, "All right, men, let's mount up!"

Smiling to himself, Radcliffe headed for his horse and then hauled himself into his saddle with a flourish. Anita, Esther, and Art Ballard were helped into the buckboard, the two women sitting beside the driver on the seat and the young man just behind them. Their luggage was then put aboard and the two troopers and the wounded Apache made to sit toward the rear. The procession started to move northward out of Apache Junction with Greg Hammond riding beside the wagon.

Radcliffe trotted his horse directly behind the buckboard. Whenever the young officer's eyes met Simino's, he glared at the Indian, and Simino glared back. For the entire length of the journey to Fort McDowell silent hatred burned between them.

Chapter Four

Spread over a dozen acres of flat, cactus-dotted land, Fort McDowell baked in the afternoon sun while blue-clad soldiers moved about the dusty military installation, carrying out their assigned duties. The compound included a number of buildings, all unpainted and weathered by the sun. Four barracks, a blacksmith shop, an infirmary, a saddle shop, a large mess hall, officers' quarters, the commandant's office, a guardhouse, various supply buildings, a small telegraph office, an armory, and a sutler's store sat within the confines of the ten-foot-high stockade fence, and most of the buildings faced the central parade ground.

The commandant's spacious log house was situated a good distance away from the other buildings and was surrounded by its own five-foot-high fence, affording a fair amount of privacy to its inhabitants—an advantage that Colonel Philip Ballard had made full use of during his family's visit to New Orleans. The colonel had been conducting an affair with LuAnn Marlowe, a beautiful blond woman who had been widowed a month before when her husband, Captain Dan Marlowe, had been killed by Chiricahua Apaches—but the affair had been going on for over a year without anyone suspecting it. To keep

31

LuAnn at the fort after her husband's death, Ballard had arranged for her to work at the sutler's store, and it had been in the back storeroom, when the proprietor was off getting supplies, that their assignations had frequently taken place. But for the past three months the secret lovers had enjoyed the luxury of entertaining each other in style and comfort, and both were wrestling with their disappointment over the imminent arrival of Esther Ballard and her two children.

Seated next to the colonel on a couch in his parlor, LuAnn snuggled close and sighed.

"What's the matter, darling?" Ballard asked solicitously, folding her tighter in his arms as he sat beside her.

"What do you think is the matter?" she retorted, pouting. "Your family's coming home today, and I'll have to content myself with back-room meetings again. Oh, Phil, how much longer are we going to have to carry on like this? I can't stand it!"

His hands stopped moving. "What do you mean?" he asked, his voice tight.

"Philip," she said, running the tip of a forefinger across his forehead and down one cheek, "you love me, don't you?"

"Of course I love you."

"Then when are you going to divorce Esther and marry me?"

Colonel Philip Ballard's mouth pulled into a thin, grim line. "LuAnn, I . . . I can't do that," he told her nervously.

The beautiful blonde seemed stung by his words. Her soft cheeks hardened as she demanded, "What do you mean you can't do it?"

Ballard released her, rose, and started to pace the floor. "If I divorced Esther, LuAnn honey, the army would take a very dim view of it." He stopped and looked at her. "Besides, you're only newly widowed. What would people think?"

Her eyes flashing, LuAnn snapped, "It's none of their business! Nor is it the army's business! What difference does it make if some fuddy-duddies disapprove of the love we feel for each other?"

His body tensing, Ballard wiped a hand across his mouth and responded, "LuAnn, you know how conservative the army is. If I divorce my wife to marry another woman, I'll lose my commission. Be reasonable, LuAnn. I'm forty-seven years old, and I've worked too hard and waited too long to become a fort commandant to throw it all away now."

LuAnn sat up and retorted, "Well I'm thirty-five, Philip, meaning I don't have too much time to waste on hopeless romances." She rose from the couch. Panic was beginning to claw at her heart as she felt her carefully laid plans slipping away from her. Until today, everything seemed to have been working out according to her scheme . . . but now Philip Ballard's words were shaking her very foundation.

She was about to speak again when Ballard said, "LuAnn, please think of yourself, if not me. It would look especially bad to the big brass in Washington because your recently deceased husband died a hero."

LuAnn's fury exploded. Striding up and down the room, she broke into a string of profane oaths. She angrily batted a vase across the room, smashing it against the wall and shattering it. The small yellow blooms that Ballard had picked earlier that morning as a welcoming gift for his wife were scattered across the floor, and the water soaked the carpet. "Hero!" she blared. "Hah! Oh, if the big boys in Washington only knew!"

Ballard came over to her and seized her by the shoulders. "LuAnn," he said, keeping his voice level, "try to calm down. Getting upset isn't going to solve anything."

She swore again and declared, "It'll take a whole lot more than a few soft words to calm me down!" Shaking her head, she snapped, "Hero! What a laugh! My dear departed husband was an egotistical glory boy who got himself killed trying to be a shining hero!"

Ballard put his arms around her and drew her to him, holding her tightly. "Well," he chuckled, "he made it, didn't he? He just didn't live to enjoy the fame."

Ballard's embrace had a calming effect on the fiery woman. Snuggling into his arms, she dug her fingernails into his back and breathed, "Dan wasn't half the man you are, darling. Oh, Phil, I can't go on like this! I love you so much! You've got to divorce Esther and marry me! Tell the big brass that she's a witch to live with. Tell them she's made your life miserable and she's hindered your work as commandant. Tell them I've proven myself a good military wife by being married to the great hero, Dan Marlowe. Tell them anything, but you've *got* to divorce her and make me your wife!"

Ballard released her and went to look out the window. He stood with his hands folded behind him, and without turning to face her, he said, "I can't tell them anything of the kind. Esther has been a good wife, and she's done nothing but back me since the day we got married."

The tension that suddenly filled the room was almost tangible. LuAnn Marlowe's entire body shook as her temper flared again. When Ballard turned around to face her, he found her brown eyes glaring at him, and her beautiful face had turned almost ugly with rage. "You're not going to do this to me, Philip! If I'm not good enough to be your wife, then I'm not good enough to be your lover!"

Ballard opened his hands and started toward her. "LuAnn, listen. You've got to understand."

"I understand, all right!" she bellowed. "I'm nothing but a plaything! You want me when it's convenient, but you don't want me to live under the same roof with you!"

"It's not like that at all!" he protested.

"Don't lie to me!" she screamed.

Ballard grasped her wrists and said, "Hush! Somebody will hear you!"

"I don't care if I am heard!" she screamed louder. "You're not going to treat me this way! Nobody makes a fool out of me!" With that, she jerked her wrists free and stormed out of the parlor into the dining room. Walking over to the sideboard, she lifted a decanter of whiskey from a silver tray and poured herself a drink. When Ballard hurriedly entered the room himself and suggested that getting drunk would not solve anything, she picked up a glass and threw it at him. The officer ducked, and it shattered against the wall, the pieces falling to the floor.

"LuAnn!" Ballard said in a hoarse whisper. "Stop it! Someone is going to hear all this noise and you'll ruin everything!" He lunged for her, but she sidestepped him and then countered by slapping him hard across the face. Adeptly he seized her, pinning her arms to her sides with his greater strength. She struggled briefly, and then their violence changed to passion as their lips met in fiery kisses. When they finally parted, they clung to each other desperately, like people who were about to be torn apart forever.

"Oh, Philip, Philip, Philip!" she gasped. "I love you, my darling! I can't live without you!"

"I can't live without you either, LuAnn," he whispered fiercely. "Every waking moment I have you on my mind—and when I'm asleep, I dream about you. You must never leave me! Please say we can go on like we have been. Please say you understand why I can't divorce Esther."

LuAnn's head was pressed tightly to Ballard's chest as his strong arms held her close. The one thing she wanted so desperately—to be the wife of a fort commandant and enjoy all its attendant prestige—lay just beyond her reach. She had the man's love, but she did not have his name. In that moment the cunning blonde made herself a vow. For the time being she would pretend to accept the fact that their illicit relationship must remain just that—but soon the one thing that stood in her way would be removed. Something must happen to Esther Ballard.

Pulling her head back and looking up into his gray eyes, she smiled faintly and put her arms up around his neck. "All right, my darling," she cooed. "I guess I should be thankful for what I have." She sighed. "At least I know your heart belongs to me. Don't worry; I won't ever leave you. I couldn't. Your little LuAnn can't live without you."

"Now you're talking sense," he said, smiling down at her.

They kissed again, and then LuAnn advised, "I must be going. Your family will be arriving soon." She looked around the room. "I really hate to leave you with this mess—"

"I'll clean it up," Ballard assured her. "You'd best be getting back to the store. We don't want you to be fired. Then you'd have no reason for staying at the fort."

"That's right," she said, affording him a big smile.

They returned to the parlor, and she picked up a shawl that she had brought with her. Then they went into the hallway, where Ballard stood behind her while she gazed into a looking glass, smoothing out her hair and adjusting her hairpins. She eyed his reflection and smiled warmly at him. Then she turned and went along the hall to the back door, with Ballard following a few feet behind her. Reaching the door, she whirled around and fell into his arms once more. They enjoyed another kiss, and when he released her, she touched his cheek and told him, "I'll count the hours until we're together again."

"As will I," he responded, his voice hoarse with desire. Philip Ballard then opened the door and stepped out onto the back porch while she remained out of sight. Over the fence he watched three troopers walk by, heading toward the supply building. As soon as they passed from view, Ballard motioned for LuAnn to come out. "The coast is clear," he said softly.

LuAnn moved quickly, stepping off the porch and darting to the gate at the rear of the yard. She blew him a kiss, passed through the gate, and was gone.

While walking to the sutler's store, the determined blonde told herself she would find a way to get rid of Esther Ballard, and then she would marry the colonel. No one was going to stop her from becoming Mrs. Philip Ballard, wife of the commandant of Fort McDowell, Arizona Territory—no matter what it took to bring it to pass.

The slanting rays of the sun were still bright when, accompanied by a large contingent of warriors, Chago returned to the scene of battle, intent on retrieving the three dead braves who had been killed by the soldiers. Among the band of Apaches was Chago's younger brother, Nachee. The resemblance between the two warriors was so great that were it not for the ever-present red vest that Chago wore, they would be virtually indistinguishable from each other from only a few yards away.

Stopping to pick up the first body they came to, Chago muttered, "Why did the white man not stay far to the east and leave the Apache to dwell on our land as we have for countless moons? How can they not expect that we will fight off their invasion?" He looked into the face of the dead brave, telling him, "You have died nobly for our cause. You knew that this might be so when you chose to fight alongside Chago for our nation. It was the Great Spirit's will that you give your life in order that your children and their children will know freedom."

The limp form of the dead Indian was draped over a pinto's back, and the warriors moved on up the road to retrieve the next one.

When they came to the place where Simino had fallen, Chago was surprised to find that the warrior's body was gone, as was his horse. Dismounting, the solemn-faced Apache leader studied the tracks in the dirt and quickly discerned the shod hooves of army horses. Following the tracks, his experienced eye led him off the road to a spot at the base of a large rock. Nachee, whom his brother greatly relied on, dismounted as well and hurried to Chago's side. Both brothers agreed that there was evidence that Simino had been picked up and placed on a horse, and the trail of dried drops of blood in the soft earth indicated that he was still bleeding at the time—and therefore alive—when the soldiers took him.

Chago turned his face toward the north. To his warriors he said, "The blue-coats have taken Simino prisoner." Clenching his jaw, he laid a hand on Nachee's shoulder and declared, "It was white soldiers who captured our father, Pakima, and tortured him to death. We must not allow this to happen to Simino." He stopped and turned, his eyes sweeping over his warriors. "We number more than twenty-five, far more than the soldiers. We must ride swiftly and catch up to the patrol before they reach the fort. Then we will ambush them, kill them all, and free Simino!"

The angry Apaches raised their rifles in the air and shouted loudly in unison. The two brothers leaped onto their pintos, fired up with the kind of determination that only the lust for revenge imparts. After instructing one of the braves to lead the body-bearing horses back to their village, Chago touched his moccasined heels to his horse's sides and then rode to the front of the band. Raising his rifle above his head in a salute, his eyes glittered as he shouted, "Death to the blue-coats! Victory will be ours, and we will rescue our brother Simino!"

With a fierce look etched on his mahogany face, Chago led his warriors as they galloped full speed across the desert.

Chapter Five

Now within a few miles of Fort McDowell, Lieutenant Greg Hammond and his weary squad pressed onward. The spinning wagon wheels and clomping hooves churned up a constant cloud of dust around them, and the blend of swirling grit, perspiring horses, wet leather, and sweat-soaked uniforms threw a heavy, rank smell over everything.

Anita Ballard and her mother sat on the seat next to Sergeant Francis O'Malley, with the older woman in the middle. The young woman's hand was in continual motion as she tried in vain to keep the dust away from her face. From time to time she glanced over her shoulder, smiling encouragingly at her brother, seated directly behind her. Sometimes she let her eyes drift farther back to the Apache, whom she was most concerned about. He sat flanked by two troopers next to the tailgate, facing in her direction, although at no time when she turned around in the seat did Simino look her in the eye. Mostly, though, her attention was focused on Greg Hammond, who rode his horse alongside the wagon and watched her with rapt delight.

A few miles to the northeast the Mazatzal Mountains lifted their rocky ramparts over the desert. Between the road and the mountains was a dense forest of piñon trees, mixed with myriad thorny mesquite shrubs and thick patches of scrub oak. When the procession reached the sandy banks of the fork where the Verde River flowed from the north to join with the Salt River, the travelers knew they were within eight miles of their destination.

Raising a dirty, blue-sleeved arm, Greg Hammond called out to his men, "The horses will fight their bits if we don't stop and let them take their fill of water, so we'll give them five minutes in midstream, and then we'll move on!" Spurring his mount slightly, he led the way into the stream, making certain that the river was not too deep to cross at that juncture.

Sergeant Francis O'Malley halted the wagon in the middle of the stream, letting the team drink their fill, while the riders encircled the wagon and allowed their horses to slake their thirst. Lieutenant Hammond guided his mount back alongside the wagon, reining in when he was again beside Anita Ballard. The lovely redhead paused in her effort to brush the dust from her dress when Hammond drew close.

The lieutenant smiled lovingly at Anita and then looked solicitously at her mother. "How are you doing, Mrs. Ballard? Not too uncomfortable, I hope."

Esther Ballard had unbuttoned the two top buttons of her high-collared dress. While she was far from portly, neither was she svelte, and she seemed to feel the heat far more than her trim daughter. Her soft flesh glistened with sweat, and she gingerly mopped her brow with a wilted handkerchief. "You're a dear boy, Greg," she told the officer. "Thank you for your concern. I admit I've had more comfortable journeys, but on the other hand, I can handle a lot worse."

Hammond smiled. "I'm glad. I wouldn't want the colonel to think I've neglected you in any way."

Esther's laugh rang gaily. "I can assure you that none

of the Ballards could ever find any fault with you. We're all much too fond of you."

Looking pleased with the words of praise, Hammond looked away from the older woman and let his eyes linger on Anita Ballard's beautiful face. "It won't be long now, darling, before we have you home," he told her in a voice filled with love.

"Am I glad," she laughed. "If we weren't, I just might jump in the river right here and now to rid myself of all this dirt."

"I think we'll *all* get us a good bath when we get to the fort, Miss Anita," spoke up Sergeant O'Malley.

"I sure hope so," came Art Ballard's voice from the bed of the wagon. "Then we'll smell better."

There was a round of laughter as everyone agreed with the colonel's son.

Soon the procession was on the move again, and no sooner did they reach the other side of the river and regain the road when the choking dust was churned up again, causing the horses to snort repeatedly. Hammond remained next to the wagon on Anita's side, and Lieutenant Radcliffe rode beside him, frequently eyeing the young woman.

Anita Ballard and Greg Hammond passed the miles talking to each other, with the officer asking about her trip east and with her asking if he missed her. They were obviously very much in love, and the expression on Esther Ballard's face indicated that she was delighted with the match.

Suddenly one of the troopers in the back of the wagon called out, "Lieutenant Hammond, the Apache's wound seems to have opened up."

Hammond twisted in the saddle in order to see Simino, and it was evident that the wound was bleeding through the makeshift bandage. Reining in his horse, the officer waited until the rear of the wagon was parallel with him, and then he kept a steady pace with the vehicle. Bill

Radcliffe did likewise, and Hammond glanced at him, annoyed that he did not stay in position at the head of the column. But Hammond said nothing, instead focusing his attention on the Indian. "Simino," he said, "we're not that far from the fort. As soon as we arrive, I'll get you to the doctor so he can stitch up the wound and stop the bleeding."

The Apache warrior nodded without expression and then asked, "What will be done with me after medicine man treats wound?"

"Well, that'll be up to Colonel Ballard," replied Hammond. "But it's my guess that the colonel may try to use you as a bargaining tool by offering to return you to your people if Chago will agree not to attack any more whites."

After a few seconds of silence Simino asked, "And if Chago not agree?"

"I don't know," admitted Hammond. "It'll be Colonel Ballard's decision."

Glowering at the Apache, Radcliffe rasped, "I'll tell you right now, I'm going to do everything in my power to convince Colonel Ballard to hang you—and the sooner the better!"

"That's enough of that kind of talk, Radcliffe!" Hammond snapped, glaring over at the other lieutenant. "The army has regulations for dealing with prisoners, so I suggest you back off or I'll be forced to whip you again!"

The younger officer snorted in derision. "You just got in a couple of lucky punches last time, Hammond. Believe me, next time it'll be different!"

Anita Ballard looked from one man to the other. "You know, I was wondering about the bruises on your face, Lieutenant Radcliffe. Just what were you two fighting about?"

"Well, Miss Ballard, I'm glad you asked," he declared hotly. "This gives me the chance to tell you something you may not know . . . which is that your boyfriend is an Indian lover. Indeed, it may be that he's wearing the wrong uniform. Perhaps he should wear his hair down to his shoulders, tie a bandanna around his head, and get himself a red vest like Chago's. Then he'd fit in with his kind!"

Greg Hammond, fire in his eyes, spurred his horse against Radcliffe's and said, "I'm warning you, Lieutenant, if you don't curb your tongue—"

Suddenly there was a thundering of hooves and a burst of gunfire as a band of Apaches came up out of a draw from two directions, their guns blazing. Almost immediately two troopers were struck by bullets and peeled from their saddles. The procession came to an abrupt halt as the soldiers prepared to do battle.

"It's Chago!" Hammond shouted as he caught a glimpse of a red vest on one of the attackers. He dove from his saddle into the wagon, pressing Anita and Esther down into the bed of the buckboard and protecting them with his own body.

Thus shielding the two women, Hammond whipped out his revolver and started shooting at the attacking horsemen. One Apache fell with a bullet hole in his forehead, but at the same instant another trooper went down, bleeding from a mortal wound. Hammond was having difficulty aiming because the wagon was swaying every which way, despite Sergeant O'Malley's best efforts to keep the team from bolting. Adding to Hammond's difficulty was the dust and gun smoke that fogged the entire area. All he knew for certain was that there was nowhere to go for cover. The Apaches had caught them in the open.

Then, just as suddenly as they had appeared, Chago and his men completed their pass and retreated out of range. Cautiously looking around, Lieutenant Hammond assessed the damage. Two Apaches lay dead on the ground, their riderless pintos following the retreating band, and another was severely wounded and slumped forward on his horse. Before Hammond could stop him, Radcliffe had pushed his own mount beside the wounded warrior, and as the Indian lifted his languid eyes, Radcliffe cocked his revolver and pointed it straight at his head.

"No!" Hammond roared, but it was too late. Radcliffe squeezed the trigger, and the gun boomed. The slug ripped through the red man's head and buried itself in the pinto's neck. The horse screamed and collapsed on the ground, where it kicked a few times, dying as blood flowed freely from an arterial wound.

Looking away, sickened, Hammond made sure the women and Art Ballard were all right and then said to them, "I want all three of you under the wagon. The Apaches will be back as soon as they regroup."

Art said excitedly, "I can use a gun, sir! Please let me have one!"

"I said I want you under the wagon!" Hammond snapped back. "Get down there and take care of your mother and your sister!"

Fear was etched on the faces of the two women as they climbed from the wagon with Art's help and crawled underneath.

Looking around at all of his men, Hammond shouted, "They've outmaneuvered us! We'll have to make a stand right here!" The young officer suddenly had an idea. Pulling a ten-foot length of rope from the back of the wagon, he ordered, "Dismount, men, and make a tight circle around the wagon. Lay your horses down and use them as shields."

As Radcliffe slid from his saddle, he scowled and asked, "Why don't we just position ourselves and shoot them like sitting ducks when they regroup and make another pass?"

Hammond regarded him with disdain. "Your tactic is based on too many textbooks and no field experience, Radcliffe. Can't you see that they far outnumber us and could easily wipe us out? Our only chance is to put Simino in a vulnerable position. Now, get your horse on the ground."

Radcliffe gave Hammond a blank look and then attempted to obey the command. The horse refused to budge.

Shaking his head, Sergeant Chuck Foster stepped beside the officer and elbowed him out of the way. "Like this, *sir*," the trooper said scornfully, locking the horse's head in the crook of his arm and giving it one good twist, forcing the animal to the ground. "What'd they teach you in that fancy school, anyhow?" the sergeant muttered as he hurried back to his position.

Walking to the rear of the wagon, Hammond told O'Malley, "Sergeant, set the brake on the wagon, and make sure it can't come loose. Then get under the wagon with the Ballards." That done, the officer noted that the last man was pulling his horse down, closing the tight circle around the wagon. He looked to see if the Apaches were coming yet, but there was no sign of them.

Hammond climbed into the wagon and stared briefly at Simino. Picking up a coil of rope, he declared, "Simino, you may be our only hope for getting out of here alive." He then called to O'Malley, "Sergeant, give me a hand here." The two men lifted the wounded Apache out of the wagon bed, and Hammond stood Simino beside one of the rear wagon wheels. As he lashed the rope around the Indian's body, securing him to the wheel, the lieutenant murmured, "It's clear that Chago has come to rescue you. So I figure if I put you where it would be easy for a stray bullet to hit you, it may very well hamper Chago's battle plan."

The warrior said nothing, and his face remained impassive.

Standing back and examining his work, Hammond nodded. The rope was wrapped several times around the Indian's chest—so that it would be very evident that he was held fast to the wagon. With Simino in such plain view, it would be immediately obvious to Chago and his

warriors that if they shot at the soldiers, they could easily
hit their brother Apache instead.

Positioning himself beside the wagon, Greg Hammond
drew his revolver and cocked it, then—as the tension
mounted—waited for Chago's return. Moments later, the
rumble of hooves met his ears and one of his men shouted,
"Here they come, Lieutenant!"

The Apaches thundered over the crest of the draw,
and in the light of the setting sun, Chago's bright red vest
looked as if it were on fire. Half the Indian force came
from the right while the remainder charged in from the
left.

"Get ready, men!" Hammond shouted. "Don't shoot
until you're sure your targets are well within range!"

Riding in the lead of one formation while his brother
headed the other, Chago drove his pinto hard. He was
bent on wiping out the whites, but when he got close
enough to begin shooting at the soldiers, he saw Simino
bound securely to the wagon. Furious, Chago signaled his
men to hold their fire, afraid of endangering his wounded
brother.

As the blue-coated soldiers raised their rifles, ready
to unleash a hail of lead at the charging Indians, the
red-vested leader jerked back on his reins. At Chago's
command the Apaches pivoted their mounts and retreated
back to the ravine. Not a single shot had been fired.

When the Indians had regrouped, Chago looked at
Nachee and glowered. Cursing the fast-thinking white
leader, he told his brother, "We cannot risk Simino's life
by shooting the soldiers—but we also cannot allow them
to take him to the fort."

Nachee agreed. "If we were to rush in and try to free
Simino, the soldiers would no doubt shoot him. Besides,
releasing him from the rope that binds him to the wagon
would take far too long."

One of the other warriors asked with impatience, "Chago, are we not letting the white devils get away from us as we speak?"

Chago briefly glanced in the direction they had come from and then shook his head. "The officer who leads them knows better than to try to escape. He realizes that even if they were to ride in formation, it would be a simple matter for us to shoot them one by one without placing Simino in danger. No, they will wait until he knows it is safe to move—especially since they are transporting two women."

Nachee then reminded his brother, "It grows late, and we cannot risk doing battle once night falls. The wise ones have always told us that souls torn from our bodies in darkness will be doomed to wander through eternity without finding their rightful resting place."

Chago snorted in derision. "I do not credit these ancient superstitions. But you are right, my brother: Some of our fellow warriors still believe in them, so we should take action quickly."

Nachee looked thoughtful for a few moments and then said, "I have an idea. Let us strike them with knives and war clubs. While the fighting is fierce, we will capture one of the whites and hold him as a ransom for Simino."

Chago nodded his head slowly. Sneering wickedly, he declared, "I like your idea, my brother. However, instead of capturing one of the men, we will capture one of the women in the group. I saw them hidden under the wagon during the last pass."

"That is even better!" exclaimed Nachee.

"Yes, I believe it will work very well to our advantage." Looking at his men, Chago continued, "While my warriors are keeping the blue-coats engaged in hand-to-hand battle, I will personally capture one of the women. Even if you are unable to subdue the soldiers, you can retreat once I have our hostage, for I can then demand a parley with the leader and bargain for a trade."

Feeling confident that Chago's plan would work, the Apaches prepared to charge.

Chapter Six

Lying behind his horse, Lieutenant Bill Radcliffe swore under his breath and muttered that were it not for Greg Hammond, he would not now be pinned prone in the dirt.

Greg Hammond stiffened. "Apparently you have something to say to me, Lieutenant," he told Radcliffe coldly. "If you can't behave like an officer and a gentleman, then at least try to act like a man and say it to my face."

Twisting around, Radcliffe glared at the older officer and snarled, "I said we wouldn't be in this fix right now if it wasn't for your love for Indians, Hammond. This whole fiasco is your fault. If you had let me put a bullet through that stinking Apache's head as he deserved, we'd all be back at the fort by now." He glanced at the young woman sheltered under the wagon and added, "I hope your Miss Ballard knows exactly what kind of a man she's gotten involved with!"

Greg Hammond felt his face burn with anger. Radcliffe had pushed him to the limit, and his fury threatened to explode—but now was not the time, for the Apaches would be back any minute. He would deal with the brash lieutenant later, though. Forcing his voice to remain level, he ordered, "Save your energy for fighting Apaches, Lieutenant Radcliffe."

But Radcliffe would not be reasoned with. His contempt for his commanding officer clearly evident, he spat, "If you hadn't stopped me from shooting that red-skinned vermin, Chago would have picked up his corpse and been back at the Apache village by now. Instead, three men from your squad are dead because you had to show kindness to this bloody savage!"

"I told you to shut up, Lieutenant!" barked Hammond.

Radcliffe shouted back, "I respectfully decline that request, sir! The fact is, Lieutenant, you refuse to face the truth—which is that your lily-livered attitude has cost good men their lives! And why? To save the life of a bloodthirsty savage who would kill us all, including Miss Ballard, if he had the chance! You know what I think, Lieutenant? I think you've forgotten where your first loyalties lie, and you're not fit to lead these men!"

Several of the troopers arrayed near Radcliffe stirred uneasily and looked at each other with eyes that said the young lieutenant had made a valid point. But Sergeant Francis O'Malley, who was positioned at the rear of the wagon, looked sternly at Radcliffe and in an angry voice intoned, "Lieutenant Radcliffe, *sir*, I would like to suggest respectfully that you halt your criticism of Lieutenant Hammond—'cause there's not a man jack among these troopers who wouldn't go to his defense . . . especially me."

Radcliffe's face tightened, and when he spoke his voice was a low growl. "Are you threatening me, Sergeant? Because if you are, I assume you know the penalty for an enlisted man striking an officer."

"Well, now, sir," O'Malley replied, drawing out the words, "you can interpret those words any way you want . . . but I will say this: Sometimes the offense is well worth the penalty! In fact—"

"Here they come!" shouted one of the troopers.

Every eye turned toward the rim of the ravine as twenty or more whooping Apaches, flattened so low on their pintos' backs that they were almost invisible, came at them. The army rifles barked, taking down two of the Indians, but when there was no return fire, Greg Hammond knew what they were planning.

Above the roar of the gunfire, he shouted, "Get on your feet, men! They're coming in to fight us hand-to-hand!"

The troopers rose up to meet the oncoming horde at the same time that their frightened horses began scrambling to their feet. Hammond's heart thudded loudly in his chest when the Apaches leaped off their pintos with their long-bladed knives flashing orange in the light of the setting sun. Suddenly there was a clash of bodies locked in mortal combat as the Apaches dove onto the soldiers.

Both sides fought ferociously. Hammond found himself doing battle with two warriors attempting to plunge their knives into his body. Through supreme effort he managed to avoid their deadly blades, but he could not inflict any damage himself; if he tried to bring his gun up into firing position and stood still long enough to aim it, his arm would immediately be slashed.

Two other blue-uniformed men fought side by side, each facing a determined foe. One trooper dodged a swinging blade and broke the jaw of his red-skinned opponent with the butt of his rifle, but the other trooper's skull was savagely struck by a war club.

The thrill of having his first face-to-face battle with the enemy surged through Radcliffe as a fierce-looking warrior came at him. The Apache swung his razor-sharp blade at the lieutenant, but Radcliffe sidestepped and brought the barrel of his revolver down on the brave's head. However, the blow was a glancing one, and it staggered the Apache only temporarily before he came at Radcliffe again.

The lieutenant was able to bring his revolver to bear, but as he squeezed the trigger, two men who were wrestling bumped into him, and the shot went astray. The Apache collided with Radcliffe, and they both went down. Whooping loudly, the Apache drew back his knife arm, then plunged the blade downward. Radcliffe, shifting his torso by inches, avoided the weapon, and the long blade was buried in the dirt. Both men scrambled to their knees, and the Apache pulled on the weapon, trying to free it, while Radcliffe attempted to wrest his hand from the weapon. Sweat beaded the lieutenant's brow as he slowly but surely lost the contest. The Indian finally wrenched the knife free, howling triumphantly.

The knife stabbed into Radcliffe's left side, and the officer sank to the ground on his back. The Indian jerked the blade out and drew back his arm once again, preparing to execute a lethal blow.

Suddenly Sergeant Foster kicked the knife from the Apache's hand, and the Indian howled with pain. Foster pounced on him, and the two men rolled in the dirt, fists flying.

Bill Radcliffe raised up on one elbow and looked at his bleeding wound. His lips quivered as he squeezed together the flaps of skin with his right hand. "I'm still alive!" he whispered exultantly. "I'm still alive!"

The considerably larger Foster managed to get on top of his foe and, locking his strong hands under the warrior's chin, gave the Indian's head a violent twist. There was a sickening sound of cracking bones, and the red man went limp in Foster's hands. Letting the dead Apache fall to the earth like a rag doll, the trooper dashed to Radcliffe, who had crawled toward the wagon and collapsed a few yards from it. Foster dragged him alongside the wagon to get him out of the immediate line of battle, and kneeling down, he began ripping the lieutenant's shirt into makeshift bandages.

Greg Hammond's agile body and fighting experience had finally enabled him to get the better of one of the braves who had attacked him, but the second warrior, wielding a war club in one hand and a knife in the other, was proving a hardier foe. After losing his revolver during the struggle, Hammond had quickly snatched up a rifle that was lying on the ground and was now using it to fend off his opponent's weapons.

The dust was swirling all around Hammond as the Apache swung his weapons, backing the officer up against the side of the wagon. Suddenly the war club smashed against the edge of the wagon bed, splintering both the wagon and the club.

Reacting quickly, the lieutenant brought up his rifle butt and caught the warrior square on the jaw with it, and the Indian staggered backward and fell, the knife slipping from his fingers. Hammond dove for the knife and, pinning his foe to the ground with his booted foot, drove the sharp point into the man's throat. The Apache gagged, and blood spurted from his mouth and the wound. He would be dead within moments. Before the Indian had even breathed his last, Hammond was racing to assist another trooper doing battle with two warriors.

With all the soldiers involved in hand-to-hand combat, Chago seized the opportunity and rode his horse into the middle of the fray. He dismounted quickly, made his way in a crouch to the wagon, and knelt beside it. After a brief look, he reached under the vehicle and grabbed hold of Anita's arm, dragging her screaming from her shelter. Although she twisted and kicked and tried to scratch at his eyes, her efforts were futile, for she was no match for his strength. He flung her over his shoulder and raced for his pinto, Anita dangling over his back and beating on his body with her fists. None of the soldiers would dare fire at him with Anita such a vulnerable target.

Just as Chago was lifting her onto his pinto's back, Greg Hammond and the Apache with whom he was wrestling shifted their positions, and the young officer saw that his woman was being kidnapped. Sudden strength surged through Hammond's body. He brought a knee up into the Indian's groin, and as the warrior howled with pain, the lieutenant delivered a haymaker to his jaw. The Apache went down hard.

Freed of his foe, Hammond bolted toward Chago, closing the final few feet between them by leaping at the Indian leader and tackling him. The move stunned the warrior long enough for Hammond to shout to Anita—mounted on the pinto's back—"Ride to the fort and bring help! Hurry!"

Anita, an accomplished horsewoman, grabbed the reins, dug her heels into the horse's sides, and galloped away. She had gone only a short distance when she saw a cavalry patrol from Fort McDowell. The troopers, coming on the run, were led by an officer whom she recognized. Anita raced toward him, shouting, "Captain Oatman! Captain Oatman!"

Captain Hal Oatman, who at forty-two was a twenty-year veteran of the army, raised his hand, bringing his men to an immediate halt. Reaching the officer's side, Anita gasped, "Our men are under attack by the Apaches! They need your help!"

Touching his hat brim, the officer assured her, "That's just where we were heading, Miss Ballard. We were returning to the fort when our course took us to a high knoll, and we saw the battle taking place."

"My mother and brother are there, too, Captain," Anita said breathlessly. "You've got to rescue them!"

"We will—but I want you to promise to stay a good distance away, Miss Ballard," the captain insisted. "Don't come anywhere near the area until it's clearly safe." Without waiting for a response, the captain ordered his men forward, and the platoon galloped ahead, weapons drawn and ready.

As the reinforcements rode toward the fray, Greg Hammond and Chago were each trying to gain advantage over the other. The Apache's knife was in his right hand as he and the lieutenant thrashed about in the dirt, rolling over and over. The young officer's uniform had been slashed in a half-dozen places where the Indian had attempted to stab him but had only nicked the thick blue material as Hammond nimbly avoided the blade.

Suddenly Chago's brother spotted the blue-uniformed riders coming from the north, and he shouted a warning to his braves. Although three more soldiers had died, the Apaches abruptly broke off the fight, knowing that once the patrol arrived, the warriors would be far outnumbered. The Indians mounted their pintos, the able-bodied assisting the wounded, and rode away. The soldiers, weary from the battle, did not pursue them.

Greg Hammond and Chago, however, were still locked in combat. The officer finally got the upper hand and was on top of the warrior, inching the Apache's razor-sharp blade toward his dark face. Gritting his teeth, the veins in his hands bulging from the strain, Hammond was victorious and sank the tip of the blade into Chago's flesh, ripping a four-inch cut just above the cheekbone.

Seeing his brother's precarious situation, Nachee turned his mount around and went to his rescue. He leaned from the animal's back and, using his rifle as a club, slammed the butt against Greg Hammond's head. Stunned, Hammond released his hold on the knife and fell into the dust.

Shouting encouragement to Chago, Nachee waited while his brother staggered to his feet and climbed onto a pinto belonging to one of the dead warriors. The two Apaches galloped away, successfully eluding the oncoming troopers.

Captain Hal Oatman and his men came thundering onto the scene of battle. Anita, who had waited until she could see the Apaches fleeing from the melee, was coming up fast behind them.

Slowly gaining his feet, Lieutenant Greg Hammond had to fight to maintain his balance as the reinforcements arrived. Seeing that most of his men were all right, the young officer called to the captain, "Go after the Apaches,

Hal! But try to take the one in the red vest alive, if you can, because I've got a score to settle with him!"

Oatman looked around at the battered, bloody survivors and asked Hammond, "Can you get to the fort all right?"

"We'll make it. You just catch those savages!"

"Okay, Greg." Turning to his troops, Oatman shouted, "Let's go, men," then spurred his horse and led the charge after the enemy.

As the patrol galloped away, Anita Ballard came riding in on Chago's pinto and slid from its back into Greg Hammond's arms. "Oh, my darling!" she exclaimed. "Are you all right?"

"I'm fine," Hammond assured her somewhat breathlessly. "Are *you* all right?"

"Yes, thanks to you," she whispered, stroking his face tenderly.

Hammond started leading Anita toward the wagon, where her brother, who had extricated himself from underneath, was helping Esther Ballard out. The young officer halted when he reached Sergeant Chuck Foster, who looked at the lieutenant and halfheartedly saluted.

"How have we fared in the way of casualties, Sergeant?" Hammond asked.

"Not too well, sir. Higgins, Richardson, and Doyle are dead," the trooper reported sadly. "Most of us are cut up some, and Gerald Blevins took a tough blow to the head with a war club. He's conscious, but I'm afraid his skull might be cracked."

Looking toward the wagon, Hammond queried, "And Radcliffe?"

"Took a knife in the side, sir, but I don't think it got any vital organs. He's bleedin' a lot, but my guess is he'll live."

Hammond nodded, saluted, and started walking toward the wagon again.

Radcliffe looked up from his prone position as Hammond and Anita approached. His pain showed clearly on his face, but even more evident was the hatred he felt for Hammond. "I hope you're satisfied!" he hissed. "Look around you, Hammond. All of this is your fault. Three more men are dead. That makes six who died after you prevented me from killing that animal, Simino." His eyes narrowed. "Rest assured, Lieutenant, the colonel is getting a full report from me!"

Ignoring Radcliffe, Hammond told the more able-bodied of his men to place the severely wounded soldiers in the wagon bed and then to untie Simino's bonds and put him back in the wagon as well.

Radcliffe gasped with pain as two of the troopers picked him up, and he passed out. The three men killed in the battle were draped over their horses' backs, joining those thus arrayed who had been previously killed.

The battered men in blue mounted up. As the two women resumed their places beside Sergeant O'Malley on the wagon seat, Greg Hammond promised them that the remainder of the ride back to the fort would be uneventful.

"I certainly hope so," Esther Ballard declared, "although I want you to know that I don't in the least hold you responsible for what happened, Greg."

From his position behind the seat, Art Ballard concurred. "You did what you felt was right, Greg."

Hammond smiled thinly. "Thanks. I appreciate your confidence."

"You have more than my confidence," Esther announced. "You have my undying gratitude for rescuing Anita from that horrible savage."

Smiling down at his commandant's wife, Hammond pointed out, "I would have done the same for any woman, Mrs. Ballard—but I suppose my love for Anita gave me even greater incentive." After a brief pause, he added, "I want you to know that I plan to ask your husband for permission to marry your daughter as soon as I have a few moments alone with him."

The look in Esther's eyes told Hammond she was

pleased, but she suggested, "I'm sure my husband is going to be upset when he hears of the casualties today, Greg. Let's give him a day to cool down. I'll tell you what. How about coming to dinner at our house tomorrow night? After dinner you and Philip can go out on the porch alone and talk."

"You just made a deal, ma'am," Hammond said, grinning. "I'll be there."

Shifting his gaze from the older woman to the younger, he saw from Anita's expression that she could not be more pleased as she returned his gaze and smiled at him lovingly.

Chapter Seven

The rim of the sun was touching the horizon as Chago and his warriors pushed their horses hard toward their village. Two wounded Apaches who had been helped to their pintos when the warriors were forced to flee were barely holding on—both were bleeding profusely and losing strength as they rode. Suddenly one of them slipped and hit the ground, landing hard and throwing up a cloud of dust.

Chago reined in and his braves followed suit. Several of them turned their horses and cantered back for their fallen brother. Suddenly one of the others pointed behind them and cried, "Chago! The blue-coats follow us!"

The red-vested leader turned and stared. A squad of soldiers was coming toward them at a full gallop. Chago cursed and then shouted to the warriors who had gone to rescue the wounded brave, "Leave Karibi! We must go now and take cover in those rocks!" He pointed at a towering sandstone monolith; around its base lay great chunks of stone that had broken off during some ancient trembling of the earth.

The warriors who had gone back for their wounded friend leaped onto their pintos and rejoined the band.

They had all just started toward the boulders when the other wounded Apache fell from his animal and landed in a crumpled heap in the dirt. Knowing they could not spare the time to help him, either, the warriors kept going, racing toward the rock formation.

Chago and his braves guided their pintos among the huge boulders and dismounted. After untying their rifles and ammunition sacks from around the horses' necks, they dashed for cover and settled in, levering cartridges into their rifles.

Nachee hunkered down beside his brother. Looking at the still-bleeding, jagged gash on Chago's face, Nachee commented, "That cut will leave an ugly scar."

Chago's eyes were full of hatred as he turned to Nachee and proclaimed in a chilling voice, "I swear by the gods that one day I will kill the lieutenant!"

Galloping in with his troopers, Captain Hal Oatman made a quick count of the Indians dashing into the rocks. He realized that the Apaches outnumbered him and his men—also, the Indians had the advantage of being in protective cover. But in spite of the odds, the soldiers had to attempt to wipe them out. Remembering Hammond's words, Oatman doubted they would be able to spare the one in the red vest for him; every one of the warriors would have to be a target for his men.

Guns ready, they charged toward the rocks.

The fiery red sun was dipping below the horizon when Hammond's battered and bloodied men arrived at Fort McDowell, escorting Colonel Ballard's family. The big gate swung open, and the patrol and the wagon—both due hours earlier—spilled into the parade ground. The other soldiers clustered around the battle-weary group and offered their assistance.

A Babel arose among the troopers as they barraged the lieutenant with questions about what had happened.

"You'll hear the details later," Hammond told them. "Right now we've got men who need medical attention, and the colonel's family needs to get home."

An earnest young corporal presented himself to Hammond, saluting smartly. "Sir, the colonel will wish to know you're back and that his family is home. Shall I run and tell him?"

"That won't be necessary, Corporal Graves. I'll escort the Ballards to the house in a moment. I need to talk to the colonel anyway."

"Yes, sir." Sam Graves saluted again, turned on his heel, and started walking away.

Easing his exhausted body from the saddle, Hammond called after him, "Graves . . ."

Halting in his tracks, the young man pivoted and asked, "Yes, sir?"

"There is something you can do. It would help if you'd run ahead and alert Captain Wheatley that we've got some wounded men here, and we'll have them at his infirmary in a couple of minutes."

"Yes, sir!" Graves turned and ran for Dr. Harrison Wheatley's quarters.

Hammond stepped to the wagon and explained to the Ballards, "Let me just see these wounded men off to the infirmary, then I'll drive you home. I know that keeping you waiting even a few more minutes is an imposition after all you've been through, but I must give at least a brief report to the colonel anyway—and I'd prefer escorting you there myself."

Esther, Anita, and Art nodded their assent and remained in the wagon.

The lieutenant put Sergeant Chuck Foster in charge of getting the injured men to the post physician, further instructing him that Simino was also to be given medical attention at the infirmary. "As soon as he's patched up, I want him placed in the guardhouse. And no one—I repeat, no one—is to attempt to retaliate in any way. If I learn that the Apache has come to harm, I will see to it that, at the very least, the offender is immediately demoted."

Foster nodded. "Don't worry, Lieutenant. I'll take care of the men and make sure Simino's safe."

Hammond then ordered some of the men who stood by to take the bodies of the dead troopers and place them in the ice house. They would remain there until there was time for a full military funeral, which would also include the troopers who had fallen in the very first melee and were being prepared for burial by the Apache Junction undertaker.

With all the priorities well taken care of, Hammond climbed into the wagon seat and clucked to the team.

Moments later the wagon rolled to a stop in front of the Ballard house. Greg and Art jumped down, and Art helped his mother out of the wagon while Greg did the same for Anita. The lieutenant held the gate open for the weary travelers.

As the four made their way up the pathway, the door opened, spilling light onto the porch, and Colonel Philip Ballard's silhouette filled the doorway. His voice was choked with relief as he exclaimed, "Oh, thank God! You're all right."

The fort commandant embraced his family and then told them that when hours had passed without their arrival, he had wired the California & Arizona office in Apache Junction to ask if the stage had been delayed. The agent had wired back, saying that the Ballards and their army escort had left for the fort a good deal earlier. When more time passed and they still had not arrived—nor had the other patrols that had been scouting the area that day— Ballard became extremely worried. He had been just about to send a search party out when he heard the wagon draw up to the house.

"Well, we have a lot to tell you, dear," Esther breathed

as she stepped inside, followed by the others, and sank heavily onto the sofa. "Greg will give you the whole story . . . or at least as much as he can before he collapses from exhaustion."

"You *all* look exhausted," commented Ballard. "What happened?"

"We found out today that Chago is back in the area—and is keen on shedding white blood to avenge his father's torture and death," Hammond began. "He and a bunch of his warriors attacked the stage your family was on." He glanced at the colonel's family, adding, "It's a miracle they're still alive. All the other passengers, as well as the stage crew, were killed."

Colonel Philip Ballard was both shocked and angered. Swinging a fist, he swore loudly. "Greg, I don't understand it. Why would Chief Amanzus allow that young hotheaded brave to break our agreement?"

Shaking his head, Hammond responded, "I don't believe it's a matter of the chief allowing anything, sir. According to an Apache warrior we have as our prisoner, this Chago has taken matters into his own hands."

"A prisoner, you say?"

"Yes, sir. Your son managed to shoot three of the braves who attacked the stage, and one of them is still alive. I decided he would serve us well as a bargaining tool, and I brought him in. Doc Wheatley is patching him up now."

"I want to talk to him," Ballard said stiffly.

"I figured you would. Anyway, we chased Chago and the rest of his bunch, and when we caught up with them, we killed all but Chago. He got away, then returned with over twenty more warriors, and they attacked us a few miles out from the fort." Greg Hammond's face became grim. "We killed several Apaches, sir, but . . . but we'd lost four men in pursuing Chago and we were seriously outnumbered. When Chago came at us again we lost six more."

"Ten men in all!" exclaimed Ballard.

"Yes, sir. The last fight was a hand-to-hand scrap in which three of our men were killed and a lot of the others came away wounded—some seriously and some superficially, but none mortally. At least I don't think so. Corporal Blevins took a pretty hard chop on the head with a war club, but I hope he'll be all right. Watson and Foley got chewed up some, too."

The colonel stroked his mustache. "Greg, I'll want a more formal and official report tomorrow from you and Lieutenant Radcliffe."

Clearing his throat, Hammond answered with some hesitation, "I'm, uh; afraid the lieutenant won't be up to it that soon, sir. He was wounded during the fray. I doubt he'll be able to give you his report for two or three days, sir."

The colonel sighed. "All right. But I want all the details from you tomorrow."

"Yes, sir."

"I am assuming you chased Chago off again."

"Not our group, sir," Hammond corrected. "Captain Oatman and his men did. They came along when we were in the thick of it, and Chago and his remaining warriors hightailed it away. I didn't wait around for Hal's—that is, Captain Oatman's—return, as I wanted to get my wounded men and your family back as quickly as possible."

"So that's why they're late," mused Ballard. "I was getting concerned about them, also. I hope they kill that blood-hungry Chago."

"Me too, sir."

Shaking his head and staring blankly out the window, Ballard whispered, "Ten men. Ten!" Turning his eyes back to Hammond, he asked, "Either of the sergeants among the dead?"

"No, sir," answered Hammond. Holding out his slashed sleeve for inspection, he continued, "They were as lucky as I was. Neither of them suffered any damage, except to their uniforms."

Ballard sighed and said, "Well, I'm glad at least for that."

Anita linked her arm in Hammond's and told her father, "Greg risked his life to save me from being kidnapped by Chago himself."

"What!" Ballard swore again. "How dare that filthy savage lay his hands on my daughter!" Looking gratefully at the young lieutenant, he asked, "Greg, how can I ever thank you for saving Anita?"

"You don't have to thank me, sir. As a matter of fact, sir, as you know, I have very strong feelings toward Anita, and I—"

"Greg is going to have dinner with us tomorrow night, Phil," cut in Esther, seizing the moment.

Ballard smiled broadly. "Wonderful!" he exclaimed. "It will be a pleasure to have you, Greg."

"Thank you, sir," replied Hammond, darting a quick glance at Anita.

Esther stood up and gestured expansively. "Well, I've got to heat some water. Three people in this family are in dire need of a bath."

The others laughed in agreement, and then the colonel ushered Hammond toward the door. "Come by when you can tomorrow, Greg, to make your report. I'll want to meet with Captain Oatman, too—I'm sure he'll be back before too long. I'll need to know how it turned out with him before we can discuss our next move intelligently. If he and his men have managed to kill Chago, it'll put a different light on our approach to Amanzus. As a matter of fact, I'll want to speak to Bill Radcliffe, too, when he's feeling up to it."

"Yes, sir," Hammond responded. "And now, if you don't mind, speaking of baths, I could use one, too."

"Do two things for me, Greg," the colonel said as he held open the door.

"Certainly, sir."

"Tell the guards at the gate that I want word brought to me the minute Captain Oatman and his men return—no matter what time it is."

"Yes, sir. And the other request?"

"Tell Captain Wheatley to let me know if any of the wounded men are in any real danger . . . or if any of them takes a turn for the worse."

Hammond agreed and was about to leave when Anita stepped between her father and the lieutenant.

"I would like a few moments alone with Greg," she announced, taking his arm.

The commandant smiled. "Certainly, my dear."

Twilight had given way to night as Greg Hammond and Anita Ballard stepped outside onto the porch. A three-quarter moon shone brightly, and countless crickets had begun their nightly concert. The tall lieutenant took the beautiful redhead in his arms and held her tight.

"I sure have missed you," he breathed softly.

"I've missed you, too," she murmured. A few seconds passed and then she said, "Thank you again, dearest, for saving me from that horrible savage."

Pulling his head back and looking into her eyes, he told her fervently, "Honey, if I had to, I'd take on the whole Apache nation to protect you. I love you more than I could ever tell you."

Anita tilted her face toward his and they kissed tenderly.

Hugging him tightly, she whispered, "Oh, darling, I'm so excited about tomorrow night! I just know Daddy will give his consent for us to become engaged."

"I sure hope so," he said, grinning. "I wouldn't want to have to desert the army so we could elope."

Anita giggled and then kissed him again.

"Well, as much as I hate to leave you," Hammond sighed, "I'd better say good night. We've both had an exhausting day."

"And a dirty one," she laughed.

Hammond walked down the pathway, pausing at the gate to wave, and then went to deliver the colonel's message to the guards. He then walked to the infirmary and left word for Captain Wheatley, the army physician, of the colonel's request. That done, Hammond headed for his quarters. A hot bath and a good night's sleep were definitely in order.

Despite having been thoroughly exhausted the night before, waking early was so automatic for the young officer that he was shaved and already dressing when the bugler woke up the fort the next morning. After leaving his quarters, Hammond walked to the gate and inquired about Captain Hal Oatman and his squad. When he was told that they had not returned, apprehension began to gnaw at Hammond's mind. Something was very wrong.

At the infirmary, the lieutenant found Dr. Harrison Wheatley cleaning instruments at a small table. An army physician since before the Civil War, Wheatley had patched up Union soldiers during the four years of that terrible conflict and had come out to the frontier shortly thereafter. He had a bushy head of silver-white hair, with eyebrows and mustache to match.

"Good morning, Doc," Hammond said as he crossed the room to where the physician sat.

"Good morning," echoed Wheatley.

Gesturing with his chin toward the closed door to the ward, the lieutenant asked, "How are your patients?"

"Fair to middling," replied the physician. "I only kept four of them in the infirmary—Radcliffe, Blevins, Watson, and Foley. The others just needed some bandaging and a good night's sleep."

"How about Corporal Blevins? Will he be okay?"

"Yes, he will—although he'll be out of commission for about a month. Watson and Foley can probably be released soon—today, I'd say."

"And Radcliffe?"

"Well, the Apache knife did a bit of damage to his insides. He's had some internal bleeding, but he'll pull through all right. Had to stitch him up both front and back—that knife went clean through him. He'll be a couple of weeks getting back on his feet."

"What about the Apache?" Hammond asked next.

"I sewed him up and sent him to the guardhouse," replied Wheatley. "He'll be okay." He shook his head, and the gesture was a combination of amazement and respect. "Those Apaches are tough. He wouldn't let me give him any laudanum, and he didn't flinch once the whole time I was stitching him up."

Hammond nodded. "They're a tough bunch, all right." Heading toward the door, he said, "Well, I'll see you later, Captain."

Wheatley looked over his shoulder. "Sure thing, Lieutenant."

With fear growing in his mind over Hal Oatman and his men, Hammond returned to the gate and was told there was still no sign of them. He decided to go to the guardhouse and check on his prisoner. The guardhouse was situated behind the long, low building that housed several offices, including the commandant's, and on either side of the guardhouse were supply buildings. Approaching the two men who were stationed at the door of the guardhouse, the lieutenant smiled and saluted them.

"Good morning, sir," the men responded in unison, returning the salute.

"I'd like to talk to the Apache," Hammond informed them.

"Sure, Lieutenant," said one, turning toward the door and unlocking it. "He might be a little testy, though. He ain't had his breakfast yet."

"Was he fed last night?" Hammond inquired as the door was swung open.

"Don't know, sir," replied the man with the key. "We weren't on duty at that time."

Hammond nodded and entered the small building. It had only two small windows, one at each end close to the crude ceiling. There were three cells, and Simino was in the farthest one. The officer stood for a moment, allowing his eyes to adjust to the semidarkness, and then walked to the Apache's cell. Simino was sitting on his cot when the lieutenant approached. Rising, he stepped to the barred door and set his dark eyes on Hammond.

Looking at the fresh bandage on his prisoner's shoulder, Hammond was pleased to see that there was no blood on it. "So you're up on your feet already," Hammond commented.

Simino nodded silently.

"Did they feed you anything last night?" asked the lieutenant.

The stoic Apache nodded again. "Your medicine man instructed that clear soup be given Simino after being brought here."

"Good. You'll probably get something more substantial for your breakfast."

The warrior cocked his head. "Lieutenant, you are kind to Simino. So was white medicine man. I do not understand. I am enemy. I have shed blood of your white brothers. All other white men have shown me hatred since coming to our land. This I expect. Why are you and white medicine man kind to Apache?"

"Some of us would like to be friends with your people," Hammond said quietly, "although I'm not sure just how friendly the colonel is going to feel toward you, since his family was on the stagecoach you attacked. I'll be talking to him later this morning about what he plans to do with you."

Simino nodded again and then said, "You do not think colonel will have me hanged?"

"No—but I could be wrong."

The Apache stared at Hammond for a long moment and then told him, "Even if Colonel hangs Simino, you have done much to save Simino's life. Much thanks."

Hammond shrugged. "We'll soon see if you have good reason to thank me."

LuAnn Marlowe's job at the sutler's store required her to report for work at seven o'clock—but it was just past six-thirty when she sneaked up to the back door of Colonel Philip Ballard's office and rapped on the door, using a coded knock.

Quick footsteps were heard heading toward the door, and then it was flung open. Ballard smiled at her and then looked to see if anyone was watching before ushering her inside.

"You look ravishing this morning," he told her as he closed the door and wrapped his arms around her.

They kissed passionately; then she held her head against his chest, playing with the buttons on his tunic. "I heard about the Apache attack on the stagecoach—and the terrible loss of your men, darling. I was appalled." LuAnn was wishing Esther had been killed by the Indians, but she kept that thought to herself.

The colonel sighed. "It's real bad—and it might be worse yet. Captain Oatman and his men gave chase to the hostiles at sunset, and they haven't returned. I'm afraid of what that means."

"You have a lot on your mind, my poor darling," she cooed, stroking his face. "I wish I could take away all your cares."

"Oh, LuAnn," he breathed, hugging her tightly, "just having your love does more for me than I could ever tell you."

"I'm glad, darling," she whispered, and they kissed again.

Holding her at arm's length, Ballard advised, "You'd better go, my sweet. I noticed Greg Hammond crossing the compound not long ago, which means he's probably going to be here shortly to make his report on yesterday's battles with the Apaches."

"Oh, all right," she sighed, and then raised up on her tiptoes and kissed him again. "But I'll be back later. You can count on it—just as I'll be counting the hours." With a coquettish wink, the alluring blonde slipped out the back door and was gone.

Chapter Eight

The Arizona sun lifted into the morning sky, promising another hot day. Lieutenant Greg Hammond left the guardhouse shortly before seven o'clock, feeling better after his talk with Simino. He was about to head toward the mess hall for breakfast when he decided to take care of the report he owed Colonel Ballard first. The commandant was an early riser, and chances were he would be in his office already. Hammond was also eager to speak with the colonel about Captain Oatman and his men.

To save time, the lieutenant decided to take a shortcut, cutting across the open area between the guardhouse and the long building housing the colonel's office. Just as he started around the corner of the guardhouse, a movement at the back door of the colonel's office caught his attention. The door was open and Captain Dan Marlowe's widow, LuAnn, was emerging.

Instinctively Hammond stopped and ducked back around the corner before she could see him. Peering cautiously around the edge of the guardhouse, he observed Colonel Ballard closing his door. LuAnn Marlowe glanced around furtively and then hastened away.

Puzzled by what he had just seen, Hammond moved

across the open area, rounded the corner of the long building to the parade ground, and approached the front door of the colonel's office.

Entering the outer office, he noted that Corporal Sam Graves was not yet on duty. Graves was not due in the office until eight o'clock.

Hammond passed through the small room and tapped on the inner door, and Ballard's voice called for him to come in. The colonel was seated behind his desk with an unlit cigarillo hanging from the corner of his mouth and a match in his hand. "Greg!" he said affably. "Didn't expect to see you so early this morning, after the day you put in yesterday. Did you get a good night's rest?"

"Not exactly, sir," answered the officer. "I had Captain Oatman on my mind. I stopped by the gate and learned that he and his men still haven't returned."

"I'm worried, too," said Ballard.

For an instant it occurred to Hammond that the colonel looked rather more relaxed than concerned at the moment, but he dismissed the thought.

Ballard scratched his match on the side of the desk and then touched the flame to the cigarillo, puffing it into life. He gestured toward the single chair in front of his desk, shaking the flame from the match as Hammond sat down. After taking his first puff and blowing smoke toward the ceiling, he picked up the pack of cigarillos and extended it toward Hammond. "Smoke?"

"No, thank you, sir. I don't use them."

"Oh," said the colonel, clearing his throat. "I probably shouldn't, either. But I guess a man has to have at least one vice, don't you think?"

Hammond nodded politely. His mind went to the picture of LuAnn leaving the office by the back door, and he found it disquieting.

"I'm glad you came early," the colonel went on. "I'll want your full report on the Apaches, of course, but that'll have to wait. Our main problem is the whereabouts of

Captain Oatman and his men. My feeling is that we should go after them. What do you think?"

"I agree, sir."

"All right, then. Right after breakfast, round up twenty troopers and then head out. I'll leave the details of the search to your discretion."

Hammond stood up and said, "I'll get right to it, sir." He started to leave and then stopped and asked, "When did you want to talk to the Apache prisoner?"

"I'll do that later," Ballard said with a wave of his hand. "Right now my mind is on our missing men."

"Do you have any idea what you might do with the prisoner?"

"No, not at this point. We can discuss it when you return."

"Yes, sir," nodded Hammond. He headed for the door and had just reached it when the colonel called, "Say, Greg . . ."

Hammond paused and turned around. "Yes, sir?"

"You be careful now. I'm expecting to see you at dinner with us tonight."

"I'll do my best, Colonel," grinned Hammond. "I'm looking forward to it myself."

Still vaguely uneasy about LuAnn Marlowe's early visit to the colonel's quarters, Hammond left the office. Finding Sergeant Chuck Foster, he told him to assemble twenty men—seventeen troopers, two corporals, and a sergeant. He specified that they all be men who had not fought in the Apache conflict the day before.

Foster saluted and said, "I'll have them ready to go as soon as they've left the mess hall, sir."

"That'll be fine. I'm headed to mess myself for a quick bite."

Half an hour later Hammond left the mess hall and headed across the parade ground where the men in blue were waiting to mount their horses. His own horse was also saddled and ready to ride. As he drew near, he saw Colonel Ballard emerge onto the porch of his office, followed by Anita. The low morning sun struck her beautiful auburn hair, highlighting it and making it sparkle. Hammond felt his heartbeat quicken.

Anita stepped off the porch and approached him. "Good morning, darling," she greeted him. "Dad told me you're about to make a search for the missing men. I hope nothing is wrong." She took his arm and walked the few remaining steps with him to his horse. When he stopped, she looked longingly into his eyes and squeezed his arm. "You be careful, Greg. I want you back here tonight. I'm so excited . . ."

Lowering his voice, he said, "All the Apaches in the world couldn't keep me from your house tonight. I love you!"

"I love you, too," she smiled, pursing her lips in a quiet kiss.

As Anita retreated to the porch of the office to stand by her father, the lieutenant turned toward his men. He was about to order them to mount up when he saw Sergeant Foster standing beside a horse. Looking for another sergeant, Hammond said to him, "I see the seventeen troopers and the two corporals, Sergeant, but where's the sergeant who'll be riding with me?"

"You're lookin' at him, Lieutenant," Foster said, his lips parting in a wide grin.

Hammond set stern eyes on him. "Wait a minute, soldier. I seem to recall ordering that fresh men be rounded up. You had a rough day yesterday, a full day of patrol during which you fought two battles with Apaches. You need some rest. Now get me another sergeant on the double."

Foster replied, "So what did *you* do yesterday, Lieutenant Hammond? Go on a picnic? How about *your* rest?"

"I've been given orders," came Hammond's tart reply.

"Yes, sir. And I suppose you wouldn't have volunteered for this mission without the orders, Lieutenant? You'd be willin' to swear to that, right?"

Hammond looked at the sergeant in exasperation, but he couldn't deny the truth of the man's words. "All right, I would have volunteered. But that's my prerogative."

"Mine, too, sir, isn't it? I mean, what's good for the goose is good for the gander, as they say. I'm volunteerin' to be your sergeant on this mission. And if you don't let me, I'll tell everybody—includin' Miss Anita—a few choice stories about your early days here at the fort. I seem to recall havin' to show you a thing or two about Indian fightin' they failed to teach you back at the Point."

Coming from almost anyone else, these words would have been insulting, but from Foster, whose eyes were twinkling in merriment and affection, they had the opposite effect. Hammond shrugged and grinned, his chocolate-brown eyes mirroring the humor in Foster's. "All right, Sergeant," he conceded, "mount up. But watch your hindsides. You're too good a man to lose!"

"Thank you, *sir!*" Foster saluted smartly.

Running his gaze over the tan faces of the waiting horse soldiers, Hammond called out, "All right, men! Mount up!"

The stalwart lieutenant settled into his own saddle and cried, "Forward, ho!"

The riders quickly formed a column of five rows riding four abreast, with Greg Hammond in the lead. They were about fifty yards from the gate when a guard in the tower called down, "Lieutenant Hammond! There's a lone rider coming in from the northwest! It's one of our men, and he looks in bad shape!"

Hammond raised a hand to halt the column behind him and shouted to the guards, "Open the gate!" To Foster he said, "Hold the men here, Sergeant."

"Yes, sir," replied Foster.

As soon as there was room to get his horse through,

Hammond plunged out of the fort and galloped toward the rider, who was bent over in the saddle and clinging to the horse's neck. As he drew up, it took a few seconds for Hammond to recognize him.

Corporal Len Ames was naked to the waist and hatless, and his trousers were torn. His hair and face were covered with blood.

Hammond pulled his mount close and took hold of the bridle on Ames's horse to stop it. Sliding quickly from his saddle, he reached up to take the corporal down. He caught the odor of charred flesh at the same instant that he saw the raw, ugly burns all over Ames's upper body. The man had been tortured with red-hot irons.

Ames clung to the horse's neck and looked at Hammond with torpid eyes. "No, please, Lieutenant," he gasped. "Don't touch me! If you touch me, I won't be able to keep from screaming."

Hammond dropped his hands so the tortured man could see he was not going to touch him. "I'll lead your horse in. We'll get you to Doc Wheatley."

"No, wait," Ames said weakly, "Better . . . better let me tell you while I can, sir."

"I'm listening."

"The Apaches . . . they forted up in a . . . big rock formation. We . . . we chased 'em and Cap'n Oatman led us right up there to . . . to try to wipe 'em out. They . . . they . . ."

"Let me get my canteen, Len," said Hammond. "You've got to have some water."

Just before turning away, Hammond saw that the blood on the corporal's head came from cuts and lacerations that crossed his scalp. Obviously he had been beaten severely, and he had lost a great deal of blood.

Returning with the canteen, the lieutenant gave Ames water without touching his body. Ames thanked him, and continued. "The . . . the Apaches had us outnumbered, sir. We were also . . . at a disadvantage

with them in the rocks. They cut us down. Two or three of
the redskins died in the fight, but the entire squad was
wiped out 'cept for the Cap'n and me. Some . . . some of
the men were only wounded at first, but Chago tortured
'em to death."

"What about Captain Oatman?" asked Hammond with
apprehension in his voice.

"He's still alive, sir. He has a bad gunshot wound in
his leg. The Apaches are holding him prisoner. They left
me alive on purpose so I could bring a message to the
fort."

"You're in a lot of pain, Len," Hammond replied
soothingly. "Let's get you into the fort. You can give the
message to Colonel Ballard and me at the same time."

"Please, sir," choked Ames, "let me finish."

"All right, go ahead."

"Chago wants Chief Amanzus's son brought to a camp
he has set up in the bottom of a canyon about eight miles
northwest of here. There's a thick stand of mesquite along
its edge. Has . . . has a big tall rock standin' among the
mesquite. Rock's shaped like an eagle's head. I think they
call it Eagle Rock. There Chago will trade Cap'n Oatman
for . . . for Simino."

Hammond's face twisted. "Did I hear you correctly?
Simino is Chief Amanzus's son?"

"Yes . . . yes, sir."

Greg Hammond was surprised. Simino had not told
him he was the son of the venerable Apache chief. Capping
the canteen, Hammond said, "Listen, Len. I'm going to
lead your horse into the fort now. Doc Wheatley will fix
you up."

Fear framed the corporal's face. "Don't let anybody
touch me, Lieutenant! Please! The pain is already more
than I can bear!"

"We'll find a way to get you settled without hurting
you, Len," Greg assured him. "You just hold on."

Leading both horses and remaining on foot, Hammond

soon had Len Ames inside the fort. Men gaped with disbelieving eyes as they gathered around, and Colonel Ballard hastened to the spot where Hammond stopped. Dr. Harrison Wheatley had already been summoned, and he hurried from the infirmary, carrying his black bag. Hammond quickly pointed out the mass of burns and said, "Doc, he's begged me not to let anyone touch him. Shall we try to get him off by getting a good hold on his legs?"

Wheatley did not answer. His gaze was fixed on the corporal's face. Ames's arms were still clinging to the horse's neck, his head leaning against it. The eyes were open but stared vacantly into space. Wheatley passed a hand over the eyes twice and then said, "You can take Corporal Ames off the horse, Lieutenant. You can't hurt him now. He's dead."

A low moan rose from the crowd. Anita Ballard stood somewhat apart but close enough to see and hear what was happening. Her hand went to her mouth and she bit down on her fingers as she looked on. Death was never easy to accept, even at an army outpost in Apache country.

As some of the men took the body of Corporal Len Ames from his horse, Greg Hammond relayed Chago's message to the colonel.

When Ballard had heard it all, he bitterly cursed Chago, Amanzus, and every Apache who ever drew a breath. His face red, he snorted, "So our prisoner is the son of Amanzus, eh? Maybe we should heat up some irons and show him what it feels like!"

Greg let Ballard's words ring in his own ears, then said, "Colonel, you don't really mean that."

The colonel was breathing heavily. "No, I don't," he admitted, but his eyes still glowed with rage.

Hammond decided to wait for the commandant to cool off a bit. After a moment he was ready to ask what Ballard wanted to do about Captain Oatman when the colonel ordered, "Greg, take your detail of men and pick up the bodies of the men Chago and his hyenas killed. You'd better take a wagon, too."

"I will, sir," replied Hammond, "but what are we going to do about getting Captain Oatman back?"

Ballard thought for a few seconds and then said, "We'll no doubt have to trade—what's your prisoner's name?"

"Simino."

"We'll have to trade Simino for Captain Oatman, but we're not going to do it at the Apache camp. I don't trust Chago, and that canyon sounds like the perfect place for an ambush. We know Chago's White Mountain warriors outnumber us; they have better than three hundred, while we're down to under two hundred. If we took enough men to protect ourselves in that canyon, the fort would be left virtually unprotected. And who's to say that the White Mountain tribe hasn't arranged to have another tribe hit the fort while our men are meeting with Chago? No, our only choice is to make Amanzus come to us."

"But sir," argued Hammond, "if we don't show up with Simino pretty soon, Amanzus and Chago are going to assume we refuse to trade. They'll kill the captain."

A crooked grin appeared beneath Ballard's salt-and-pepper mustache. "Ah, but we've got an edge," he countered. "Simino is Chief Amanzus's son, and I know Amanzus. He won't endanger his own son's life by killing Oatman."

Hammond persisted. "Maybe not, sir, but if you want my opinion, I think Chago is a madman—I could see it in his eyes when I fought him yesterday. He can't be expected to behave rationally. He might just go berserk and kill Captain Oatman out of hand, regardless of the consequences."

Colonel Philip Ballard arched his back and squared his jaw. "Greg, I appreciate your concern for Hal, but I've made up my mind. We simply cannot jeopardize our fighting forces or leave the fort unprotected. We have no choice in the matter. If he wants his son, Amanzus will come to us."

Hammond bit down on his lower lip. He knew what

the colonel was saying was true. The young lieutenant's thinking was colored at the moment by the emotions that were churning inside him. The sight of Corporal Len Ames's tortured body and agonizing death had touched him deeply, and he had been thinking of what would happen to Hal Oatman if Chago was riled.

"Get your detail ready to move out with the wagon," Ballard said. "On second thought, make that two wagons. I'll get some men to start digging graves."

Greg Hammond saluted his commanding officer and obeyed.

At the Apache camp in the canyon below Eagle Rock, Captain Hal Oatman was stretched out on the ground, his wrists and ankles secured to stakes. The Apaches had stripped him to the waist, and in the harsh sunlight his lean body was shiny with sweat. An Apache medicine man had torn back his left pantleg and then crudely bandaged the bullet wound in his thigh, omitting the application of any soothing herbal remedies that might have eased the pain.

Chief Amanzus stood over Oatman, looking down at him with sad eyes. Beside the white-haired old man was the muscular Chago, and next to Chago stood Nachee, the two brothers looking almost like twins.

Since his capture, Hal Oatman had been given no food or water, and the blazing Arizona sun was mercilessly sucking the moisture from his body. His lips made a dry, smacking sound as he looked up at the chief and said, "Please, Amanzus, may I have some water?"

Before the elderly chief could speak, Chago dug his foot savagely into Oatman's ribs and cursed him, growling, "No water for white-eyes pig!"

Other warriors who were gathered around laughed, urging Chago to kick the white man again. Grinning wickedly, Chago kicked Oatman several more times, and each time the captain gritted his teeth in an attempt not to

cry out, for the Apaches would respect him more if he did
not show his agony.

Chago was about to deliver another kick when Amanzus
spoke in a low voice and said, "That is enough, Chago.
Give him some water."

The red-vested warrior glared at the chief. "Give him
water?" he repeated, as if he had not heard correctly.
"Did you say give him water?"

"I did," came Amanzus's level reply.

In the Apache nation men did not become chiefs by
inheriting the position from their fathers. They were elected
by the people, who chose their leaders for their intelligence,
fighting prowess, and leadership ability. Often the son of a
deceased chief would be favored for election, but the
succession was not automatic.

Though Amanzus was already elderly when Chief
Pakima—Chago's father—was killed, he had been chosen
because of his wisdom and natural sense of authority. He
had proven his fighting skills as a younger man, but with
age Amanzus had lost his lust for battle. He also realized
that the Apaches were losing in their struggle to drive the
white men from their land. The wise old chief knew the
whites had come to stay, and he had negotiated peace
with Colonel Philip Ballard to keep his people from being
annihilated.

Young Chago, a born leader like his father, was fast
becoming a champion among people of the White Mountain
tribe because he argued convincingly that the whites could
still be driven out. Amanzus could feel his own influence
over the people slipping away, and he saw a day approaching
when the fiery-eyed Chago would try to take control and
become chief.

If Chago refused to obey Amanzus's command to give
water to Captain Oatman, it was going be a test of the
older man's authority. What would the warriors do? Though
the people were caught up with Chago's charisma, they
still held a degree of respect for the aging chief. Amanzus
would now learn just how much respect.

Looking the young warrior in the eye, Amanzus repeated his command.

Chago, returning his stare, grunted, "I say the white soldier gets no water."

As Chago looked around to see the reaction on the faces of the warriors, Amanzus kept his tired eyes on Chago. No one spoke; not one man raised his voice in support of Amanzus or in rebuke of Chago for defying the chief. Amanzus, suddenly feeling older, could see a look of confidence spreading over Chago's face.

Amanzus said in a low voice, "You have much to learn, my young friend. You will not believe it, but I will tell you just the same: The whites will one day dominate us completely. They keep coming from the east like countless raindrops falling from the sky. Soon their fighting men will outnumber us and drive us onto reservations, captives in our own land. To antagonize the whites now will only make it harder on our people in the future."

Narrowing his eyes, Chago said, "You are right when you say I do not believe it. I say the white men can be beaten! We sent many to the white men's hell yesterday!"

"Not without loss of several of our own," parried Amanzus, "including my son, wounded and now the captive of the white man. You have disturbed me deeply, not only by what you have done to my son, but by breaking my sacred word to Colonel Philip Ballard."

"I have no wish to disturb you, Chief," said Chago. "I respect you, and I am going to get Simino back for you. But it is my belief that your soft approach to the whites is wrong. We must fight them and kill them, for only when they are dead will they not be a burr in our skin."

Amanzus now knew where he stood with the warriors. He would have no support in any attempt to negotiate another treaty with Ballard, and he would have to go along with Chago, who seemed to have the sympathy of all the White Mountain Apaches.

Chago stepped closer to Oatman so that he cast a

shadow over the captain's face; then he moved just enough to allow the piercing sun to stab the captive's eyes once again. Towering over the helpless soldier, Chago said harshly, "You better hope your friends at the fort come with Simino, Captain. I mean, you better hope they come soon."

Ignoring Chago's words, Hal Oatman rolled his tongue in his dry mouth. "Chago, what . . . makes you so brutal? Do with me what you please . . . but why did you have to torture my men to death?"

Chago pointed at the ragged cut that Greg Hammond had inflicted on Chago's face. The Apache medicine man had stitched it up roughly, and the crude threads were visible amid the small streaks of dried blood. "Do you see this?" he spat. "I have powerful hatred in my heart for man who did this! He is lieutenant with dark brown eyes and curly hair. He is still free. Because I cannot torture him, your men suffered and died in his place."

"Do you call that fair?" pressed Oatman. "It was not my men who cut your face."

"Fair?" spat Chago. "Who says what is fair? Is it fair that white people come onto our land? Is it fair you put us in bondage, as is your plan?"

Oatman made no reply. Chago bent low and said, "What is lieutenant's name—the one who cut me?"

The captain remained silent. "His name!" Chago demanded again. "Give it to me!"

Oatman whispered, "I will tell you if you will give me water."

Chago's eyes went wild. Kneeling down, he slapped Oatman's sweaty face, then said, "You are difficult to deal with, Captain."

Rising, Chago went to his horse and reached into the sack that was tied to its neck. He produced a tin cup, then went to the pack horse that bore two small wooden water barrels and poured the cup full. Returning to stand over Oatman, he sloshed the water in the cup, spilling a few drops.

Lust for the cool liquid showed in the captain's bleary eyes as his tongue ran hungrily over his dry lips.

Smiling down at him, Chago said, "You want water? Tell me name of lieutenant."

"Hammond," came the response. "His name is Greg Hammond."

"Greg Hammond," Chago echoed bitterly, the fire of hatred blazing in his eyes. "Greg Hammond."

Holding the cup of water delicately, he knelt down and said, "Captain, your greatest wish at this moment is for water, is it not so?"

Oatman pulled his lips tight and nodded with short, jerky movements.

"I thought so," said Chago as all the other Apaches looked on. "Do you know what *my* greatest wish is, Captain?" His glittering eyes bulged. "It is to put knife in your Lieutenant Greg Hammond's heart!"

The canyon was as still as a tomb, except for a slight breeze that whispered against its stony walls. Smiling devilishly, Chago glared at the white man and said, "Do you know what my second greatest desire is, Captain? Let me tell you. My second greatest desire at this moment is to drink this cup of cool water."

Watching Hal Oatman's face twist in an agony of desire, the red-vested Apache leader drank the cup of water, deliberately letting tiny drops fall from his chin uselessly onto the ground.

Chapter Nine

When Lieutenant Greg Hammond and his mounted troopers reached the site of the battle that had taken place between Chago's and Oatman's men, a strong stench assaulted their nostrils. The bodies of the dead troopers, stripped of their uniforms, lay side by side in drying pools of their own blood. It was evident that some of them had not died from their gunshot wounds, but had been given deep cuts all over their bodies so that they would bleed to death. Those whose bodies were untouched had apparently died in the battle, and Chago and his men had not bothered to mutilate them.

As Hammond swung his right leg over the saddle and dropped down, he felt queasy, and he noted the pallid, drawn expressions on his troopers' faces. "All right, men," he said grimly, "let's get them picked up. I don't see their uniforms anywhere; I guess the Indians took them."

He watched as Sergeant Chuck Foster moved close to the bodies, directing the wagons to be pulled alongside them. He was grateful that Colonel Ballard had thought to have him bring two wagons. It seemed fitting that the fallen troopers' bodies be laid out in the wagon beds so that each would have its own place, without touching another one.

Just as the wagons were brought into position, Sergeant Foster uttered a string of profanities, bringing the others in a hurry to see what had upset him. Foster pointed: The troopers who had been tortured had also had the tips of their fingers sliced off and their tongues cut out, and the bloody remains lay in a small pile beside each man's head.

Two of the men gagged and ran from the scene, while the others paled and turned away.

Greg Hammond was breathing hard. He could feel the skin of his neck and face turning hot as a flush worked its way upward, and his whole body trembled with fury. "This is barbaric!" he almost shouted. "Absolutely barbaric! These Indians may be fighting for their land, but this kind of torture is despicable! It's Chago's work, and I'm going to kill the filthy devil with my own hands! Do you men hear me? I'm—"

Sergeant Foster approached and laid a hand on Hammond's quivering arm. "Sir," he said quietly, "I know it's bad, but you need to keep a grip on yourself. You're an officer, and the men need your strength."

Hammond looked around sharply at the sergeant, ready to lash out, and then checked himself. "You—you're right, Sergeant," he said, rubbing his temples with his fingertips. "I'm sorry. It's just that . . . well, there's no excuse for barbarism like this. Chago will pay, mark my words."

"I understand, sir, but for now all we can do is load up the bodies and head back for the fort."

"Yes, of course," Hammond agreed. Turning toward the men, he said, "Let's get them into the wagons."

The soldiers quickly laid the bodies of the dead troopers in the wagons and placed tarpaulins over them. Then Hammond called for his men to mount up, and they headed for Fort McDowell.

When they arrived at the fort, the bodies were hastily

prepared for burial. At the cemetery, which was situated just outside the stockade wall to the southeast, graves had been dug not only for the fallen men in Oatman's unit but for all who had been slain by the Apaches, including those brought out from Apache Junction for final interment.

Except for the wounded men in the infirmary, the Apache prisoner, and the guards at the main gate, everyone in the fort attended the funeral. As no chaplain was present, Colonel Ballard led the service, reading from the Bible, and then he asked Hammond to say a few words.

As Hammond complied, praising the fallen men's valor as well as expressing sorrow over their loss, other emotions were stirring within him. He felt anxiety over the fate of Captain Hal Oatman. He had a nagging suspicion that the widow of the other captain might be carrying on an affair with his commanding officer. But above all, he felt hatred for the red-vested Apache who had committed such vile atrocities against soldiers of the United States Army.

With all of these emotions churning inside him, he glanced at the lovely Anita Ballard, who stood beside her parents and brother. The sight of her calmed him, even as it saddened him. She was dressed in black, and her creamy-white skin looked softer than he had ever seen it. She was beautiful, a vision of loveliness in the midst of all the horror and misery surrounding him, and he was consoled by the fact that she loved him—that tonight he was going to ask her father for her hand in marriage.

When Hammond finished speaking, seven somber-faced men under Sergeant Chuck Foster's command raised their rifles and fired three volleys. After the twenty-one-gun salute to their dead comrades, the men and women of the fort stood in silence as the bugler sounded taps, the long, drawn-out notes echoing across the landscape. Hammond felt the sadness of them touch the very depths of his soul.

When it was over, the lieutenant spoke briefly to Anita and told her he would see her for dinner at seven.

For a moment he was afraid that she might wish to postpone the evening's plans in view of the day's events and the funeral, but to his relief she confirmed that he should come that evening as arranged.

The lieutenant then proceeded to the guardhouse, where he found Simino sitting on his bunk. As the Apache recognized Hammond, he rose and stepped to the bars.

Without ceremony Hammond asked point-blank, "Why didn't you tell me you were Chief Amanzus's son?"

Surprise registered in the Indian's dark eyes. He waited a few seconds and then replied, "What purpose would be served? I do not see that Simino's being son of chief make any difference."

"That makes you more than an ordinary warrior," said Hammond. "In a situation like this it's important for us to know these things."

Simino's brow puckered. "How did you learn Amanzus is my father?"

"The hard way, believe me. Do you remember the squad of soldiers that came while we were fighting hand to hand with Chago's men?"

"Yes."

"Well, they followed Chago and attacked, but they were outnumbered. All who were not killed in the battle were tortured to death in . . . a horrible way."

Simino made no reply, but the lieutenant could see something like sympathy flickering behind his dark eyes.

"Only Captain Hal Oatman and one trooper, also wounded, were left alive," Hammond continued. "Both were wounded, but Chago did not kill them because he had other purposes for them. He tortured the trooper till he was close to death, then put him on his horse and sent him here with a message. It was that trooper who told me you were Amanzus's son."

"What was message?" queried the Apache.

"Chago and your father want to trade Captain Oatman for you."

"Will your colonel make trade?"

Greg Hammond sighed, and said, "Right now that's in question."

"Why?"

"Your father wants the trade made at the canyon by Eagle Rock, but Colonel Ballard is afraid of an ambush."

"He does not trust my father?"

"I think it is more that he does not trust Chago."

Simino nodded silently.

"Certainly you can understand that."

Simino repeated his silent nod.

"So we're waiting for Amanzus to come to us," continued Hammond. "When he does, Colonel Ballard is going to insist on a neutral place to make the trade, a place where the surroundings do not lend themselves to an ambush."

"I believe my father will agree to that, Lieutenant Greg Hammond. Amanzus wants no bloodshed between our people and whites."

"Has he no control over Chago? Or *you*, for that matter?"

"My father is old, Lieutenant Greg Hammond. Little fight is left in him. Chago is strong. Chago makes warriors believe that whites must be run off Apache lands. But if *all* white men were men like you, Simino would not mind if whites lived on Apache lands. Men like you do not make war against Apaches if Apaches do not attack you."

"You're right about that, Simino," said Hammond. "I'm not a soldier because I want to kill. I'm a soldier because I want to *prevent* killing." He paused a moment and then gritted his teeth. "There is one exception: I *do* want to kill Chago for what he has done. But even that's in line with my duty as a soldier, for Chago will go on slaughtering innocent people as long as there's breath in his lungs. He is a devil beast."

Simino made no reply, but again he nodded slowly. Then he said, "Simino is pleased that *you* are kind of man you are, Lieutenant Greg Hammond. Much thanks again that you did not let other lieutenant kill me."

Hammond lifted his hat and ran his fingers through his thick mop of dark, curly hair. "I was just following army procedure, Simino. I said at the time that the United States Army does not make war on wounded men."

Hammond was looking into the Apache's deep, black eyes. Suddenly they seemed to grow warm . . . almost friendly. Never had a hostile Indian looked at him in that manner before. "I'm glad I was able to keep Lieutenant Radcliffe from killing you, Simino," Hammond said. "I . . . sort of like you."

This time a real smile tugged at the corners of the Apache's mouth.

"I'll let you know how things develop between my colonel and your father," Hammond added, heading for the door.

When he reached it and pulled it open, the dark-skinned man called from his cell, "Lieutenant Greg Hammond . . ."

"Yes?"

"I sort of like you, too."

From the guardhouse Hammond moved through the heat of the afternoon sunlight to the infirmary. As he entered, he saw Doc Wheatley working at a table, measuring out little metal dippers of white powder and placing them into small envelopes.

Looking up, the doctor said, "Well, if it isn't the pride of Fort McDowell! Mrs. Hammond's little boy, Gregory . . . the army's proud specimen of red-blooded American manhood!"

Though ordinarily stiff and serious, Doc Wheatley was unpredictable, and every once in a while he liked to banter. Hammond was the usual target of his joshing, and the lieutenant was used to it by now, figuring that the old doctor's rough wit was a shield against the horrors of his profession. At such moments, of course, the doctor's rank of captain was forgotten.

"Flattery will get you nowhere, you old coot," Hammond teased back.

"It's flattery, all right, my boy," grinned the silver-haired physician. "Someone once said that flattery is only soft soap, and you know that soap is ninety-nine percent lye. There's a little play on words there, but I think even a low-life lieutenant can get it."

"I get it, sawbones, though I don't want it," chuckled Hammond. He tried to think of some further rejoinder but gave up the effort. The doctor always got the better of him in the end. "Actually," he said, "I'm here to see your patients. Is that all right with the learned doctor?"

"I've already released Watson and Foley, but I suppose you can see the other two," Wheatley muttered, going back to his powders. "Just don't rile them."

"I wouldn't think of it," responded Hammond, and moved into the back room.

Gerald Blevins was sitting up in his bed, reading a book. Bill Radcliffe was lying flat on his back, snoozing.

Blevins lowered the book and smiled. "Good afternoon, Lieutenant. One of these days I think you and Doc Wheatley may come to blows."

"I hope not," Hammond chuckled. "I don't believe I could whip him."

Bill Radcliffe stirred at the sound of the voices.

Standing over Blevins's bed, Hammond said, "You're looking better. You've got some color in your face."

"I am feeling better, sir," said Blevins. "Headache's about gone, and I feel stronger."

"Great!" exclaimed the lieutenant.

The wounded trooper's countenance took on a sad look. "I was sorry to hear about Captain Oatman's squad, sir. Doc told us. D'you think we'll get the captain back?"

"No thanks to the lieutenant if we do!" interrupted Radcliffe, now fully awake. "It's his fault this whole thing happened! I hear you spoke some words over the dead men at the burial, Hammond. Did you tell them you were sorry for getting them killed?"

Hammond gave Radcliffe an exasperated glance and said, "Look, Bill, I just came in here to see how you two guys were doing. I don't need—"

"They also told me the colonel read from the Bible!" cut in Radcliffe. "Did he read the part about an eye for an eye and a tooth for a tooth? If you had let me have an eye for an eye with your pal Simino, most of those soldiers out there in graves would still be alive and Captain Oatman wouldn't be in the clutches of the Apaches!"

Regarding him coolly, Hammond asked, "Don't you sing any other song, Radcliffe?"

"Sing?" rasped the redhaired man, raising himself on an elbow. "I'm gonna sing, all right! To the colonel! I'm gonna see that you're run right out of the army!"

Shaking his head in disgust, Hammond turned to leave the infirmary. At the door he glanced back at the two men. Radcliffe had lain down again and turned his face to the wall. Gerald Blevins, gesturing in the lieutenant's direction, shook his head disparagingly and then shrugged.

Shortly after seven Greg Hammond joined the Ballard family at their dinner table. Esther and Anita had prepared a beautiful meal and had decorated the table with desert flowers and colorful napkins.

In light of recent events the mood at the table was

somewhat subdued, though Art Ballard, who greatly admired Hammond, peppered the lieutenant with questions about soldiering.

Greg replied fully but distractedly, concentrating most of his attention on Anita, who was wearing a fetching cream-colored dress with lace at the collar and full, puffy sleeves. Her long auburn hair lay on her shoulders in thick curls that shone in the light of the candle chandelier above the table.

The food was delicious, and Hammond enjoyed it, but he was also a bit nervous, knowing what was to follow.

When the meal was finished, Greg said, "Ladies, that was the best dinner I have ever had. You are both excellent cooks."

Esther thanked him for his compliment and then pushed her chair back and stood up, saying, "Well, Phil, why don't you and Greg go out on the porch? Get yourselves some fresh air. It should be cooling down out there now."

The rest of them rose to their feet and Art said, "Yeah! I'll go with them."

"Oh, no you don't!" Esther said quickly. "Tonight, young man, you are going to help your sister and me do the dishes!"

"But, Ma—" the youth started to protest.

"Not another word," Esther commanded. "Come on, let's get to work."

As the colonel led him outside to the front porch, Greg Hammond's stomach seemed to be crowding his throat. Several wicker chairs were arranged in the dim light, and Ballard pointed to one of them. "Grab a seat, Greg," he said.

"Thank you, sir," said Hammond, moving to the chair.

Ballard settled into the chair next to him and pulled out a pack of cigarillos. Extending them toward Hammond, he said, "Smoke?" Then quickly he remembered. "Oh, that's right. You don't use them."

While the colonel was placing a cigarillo in his mouth and fishing through his pockets for a match, Greg said nervously, "I . . . uh . . . I'm glad we can have a few moments together alone, sir. There is something I would like to discuss with you."

"Army business can wait until tomorrow, Greg," responded Ballard. "In fact, why not stop at my office first thing in the morning—seven would be fine—to give me that detailed report on your battles with the Apaches. We never got to it today, for obvious reasons."

"I'll be there, sir," nodded Hammond, looking at the colonel in the vague light. "But what I want to discuss with you is not army business."

"Oh?" Ballard struck the match. The brief flash of light illuminated his face and then the flame ignited the end of the cigarillo. As Ballard took a puff, Greg thought the tip of the cigar resembled a single red eye glaring at him in the semidarkness.

"No. You see, sir, what I—"

"Colonel Ballard! Colonel Ballard!" An excited voice came out of the dark as hurried footsteps became louder and a shadowy figure drew near to the porch. As he came closer, both the colonel and Hammond recognized him as one of the guards from the front gate.

"What is it, Reynolds?" asked Ballard.

"It's Chief Amanzus, sir! He's at the gate with a whole bunch of his warriors, and he wants a powwow with you!"

Greg Hammond's heart sank. He had worked up the courage to ask the colonel for Anita's hand, and now this interruption had come. At the same time, however, he was as anxious as the colonel to meet with Amanzus.

"See what I told you, Greg?" said Ballard confidently. "The old boy has come to us. Let's go have a little chat with him. We'll have Hal Oatman back real soon."

Suddenly Esther, Anita, and Art appeared at the door. "What's going on?" asked Esther.

"It's Amanzus," Ballard told her. "He's here to parley."

As his family watched, Ballard and the lieutenant stepped off the porch and followed Reynolds. By the time they had crossed the darkened parade ground and reached the gate, word of what was happening had spread through the fort, and a crowd of soldiers was already gathering. Every man was carrying a weapon.

Lanterns were hung in the tower and on the stockade wall about the gate, and as soon as the gates had been opened at Ballard's order, a crowd of mounted Apaches could be seen outside, some two hundred in all by Greg Hammond's estimate. Amanzus was at their head, flanked by Chago and Nachee.

The colonel stepped through the gate, Hammond at his side, and the two halted in front of Amanzus.

Glancing over at Chago, Hammond noted the jagged gash on the Indian's cheek, quite visible by the lanterns' light. He could not help feeling some satisfaction that he had put it there. Chago returned his gaze with hate-filled eyes.

"I understand you want a powwow," Ballard said to Amanzus.

The aging Apache chief looked down at Ballard through dark eyes surrounded by wrinkles. "Yes, Colonel Philip Ballard. I want agreement to exchange your captain for my son."

"All right, we'll talk about it, Amanzus," said Ballard. "But first, tell me one thing: Why have you violated our peace treaty? Why, as I was told by your son, do your warriors plan to go on killing white people?"

The old Indian held his voice steady as he replied, "I am sad to say, Colonel Philip Ballard, that some of our young warriors are getting out of control. For this I apologize. The blood that has been shed has not been of my choosing, or of my will."

A cold smirk formed on Chago's shadowed features.

"Are you going to put a stop to it?" Ballard pressed the chief.

"I will do my best," said Amanzus, in a weary voice. Changing the subject, he asked, "What is the condition of my son?"

Hammond spoke up. "He is doing fine, Chief. I was with him this afternoon. The bullet that hit his shoulder did some damage, but he will heal eventually and be as good as new."

Ballard quickly followed up. "What is the condition of Captain Oatman?"

"He has a bullet wound in his left leg," replied Amanzus.

"His left leg? Is that all?"

"Yes. He will not die from his wound." Amanzus shifted on his mount. "We sent your soldier with message that we wanted Simino back today at Eagle Rock canyon. Why did you not bring him?"

"I'm willing to make the trade, Chief," responded Ballard, "but I want it on neutral ground, and where there is no opportunity for ambush."

Amanzus raised his heavy eyebrows. "You not trust me?"

"Let's say I do not trust those young warriors you were telling me about."

For some minutes the two leaders discussed the time and place for the exchange, finally agreeing to meet at three o'clock the next afternoon at a point midway between the fort and the Apache village. That particular spot, near a small spring, offered no cover for an ambush party. Some mesquite bushes and boulders were scattered about, but there was no way a large band of men could be concealed nearby.

"You are satisfied with the arrangements?" concluded Ballard.

Amanzus nodded.

"All right," said the colonel. "Lieutenant Greg Hammond, here, will be in charge of the exchange for our part. He will have fifty men with him. I ask, Amanzus, that you have no more than that."

"I also will send fifty men," said Amanzus. "Chago, who is here on my right hand, will be leading them."

Greg Hammond felt his blood run cold when he heard this. Risking insubordination—but knowing the colonel would be sympathetic to his wishes—he spoke up. "With all due respect to you, Colonel, and to Amanzus, there is no way I can deal with Chago. I do not hesitate to tell you both that I regard Chago as a bloody barbarian. If you want your son back, Amanzus, you will have to put someone else in charge of the exchange, or, Colonel, I'll ask you to send someone else in my place."

Anger filled Chago's obsidian eyes, but he remained silent. Simino's rank and popularity among the Apache would make it unwise to interfere in any way with the negotiations for his release.

After a moment of tense silence, as Amanzus stared at the colonel and Hammond, the old chief finally spoke. "It will be as you request, Lieutenant Greg Hammond. I will assign Nachee, who is at my left hand, to be in charge of the exchange."

Hammond was not too pleased to have Chago's brother to deal with, but he knew he had pushed the matter as far as he could.

Satisfied with the agreement, Amanzus led his warriors away into the night as the two officers returned to the fort. The gates were closed, and the soldiers started toward the barracks, while Ballard and Hammond walked toward the colonel's porch. Greg thanked the colonel for his understanding in the matter of his refusal to meet with Chago, but the colonel dismissed the matter with a wave of his hand, perceptible by the light of the moon rising above the stockade.

With the crisis over, Hammond was impatient to resume his earlier talk with the colonel, but as they approached the house they found Esther, Anita, and Art awaiting them, and the colonel took some time to fill them in on what had happened. Finally he turned to Hammond. "Let's see, Greg, you were just broaching a subject you wanted to discuss with me when we were interrupted."

"Uh . . . yes, sir," said Hammond.

Esther quickly spoke up. "Come, Anita, Art. Time to leave the men alone. Back in the house with you."

When they were gone, the two men sat down. Eager to get it over with, Greg blurted, "Colonel, sir, I am deeply in love with your daughter and I want your permission to marry her."

"You have it," came the ready reply.

There was a long pause. "I . . . do?"

"Certainly. I've been watching you two, and I think you're a perfect couple. I had a pretty strong feeling that you wanted to discuss marriage tonight; as a matter of fact, I had expected you to approach me before now."

Hammond was stunned to find it so easy. "Well, sir, I want you to know that I'm very glad you approve. I plan to make the army my career. I'm hoping to make captain before too long, and my ultimate goal is to become commandant of a fort. I hope you'll agree that I can provide well for Anita and whatever children may come along."

"I have no doubt that you will be a good provider, Greg," said Ballard with a grin, "even though the army will never make you a rich man. Believe me, I know that for a fact. I'll be proud in any case to have such a fine officer and gentleman as my son-in-law."

At that moment, the door flew open and Anita dashed to her father, wrapping her arms around him. "Oh, Daddy!" she exclaimed. "You've made me so happy! Greg and I are very much in love, and it means so much to me that you like him so well!"

Ballard embraced his daughter as Esther and Art put in an appearance. All three had obviously been listening behind the door. Art grabbed Greg's hand and pumped it, heartily welcoming him to the family, while Esther embraced her daughter. Then Esther gave Greg a hug. Finally Hammond, his arm around the woman he loved, told the family that he and Anita would set a wedding date soon.

The colonel then sat everybody down, and in front of Esther and Art he gave the young couple a lecture on the sanctity of marriage and the seriousness of the vows they would take at their wedding ceremony.

As he listened, Greg thought of LuAnn Marlowe leaving the colonel's office by the back door. He could not forget the furtive look on the widow's face as she had slunk away. Listening now to his prospective father-in-law's talk about the sacredness of marriage, Hammond tried to believe that the situation only *looked* illicit; there had to be some reasonable explanation for Mrs. Marlowe's having been with the colonel so early in the morning. He pushed the matter from his mind, dismissing it as a misunderstanding on his part.

Ballard reminded Hammond of their appointment in the morning, adding that he wanted to hear Lieutenant Radcliffe's version of the Apache incidents when Radcliffe was up to it. Then he looked around at his wife and son and said, "I think Greg and Anita would like to be alone."

Everyone rose, and Greg held Anita loosely while the Ballards bade him good night and filed into the house. When they were gone, Anita slid deeper into his arms and said softly, "Oh, Greg, I am so happy! I love you so much!"

Their lips came together in a warm and vibrant kiss; then they sat down in the wicker chairs and talked of their future. They discussed Greg's army career and his goal of becoming a commandant himself one day. The subject shifted to the family they would raise and how many children they would have. Anita already had names picked out for two boys and two girls, and Greg laughed, wondering aloud whether women began planning such things when they were still little girls playing with dolls.

They talked of a wedding date and agreed to settle it within the next few days. Hammond stood up. "Well, Miss Anita Ballard—soon to become Mrs. Gregory L. Hammond—I'd better let you go in. I've got a big day tomorrow."

Anita rose to her feet and moved into his arms again. "We're going to have a wonderful life together, darling," she said.

He squeezed her silently as the silver light of the moon poured down on them, in seeming approval of their union.

Chapter Ten

Greg Hammond awoke to the sound of rain tapping on the roof of his quarters. Rolling over in bed and opening his eyes, he saw through the two windows of his room that the cloudy sky was barely light. A sheen of raindrops was trickling down the windowpanes.

The rain was a welcome sight. It seldom lasted for very long in the desert, and its cool freshness always provided a pleasing break to the dry weather.

One habit that Hammond had developed early in life was always to be on hand a few minutes ahead of any appointment. Accordingly, at six-forty he stepped out of his quarters onto the porch and looked across the muddy parade ground at the colonel's office. Deciding that twenty minutes might be a little too early, he leaned against one of the posts and sniffed the sweet smell of the rain.

Men were moving about the fort, hurrying a little faster than usual in order to get out of the rain. The fort's post office was two doors away from the colonel's office, and Hammond saw Sergeant Francis O'Malley, who was in charge of the mail, come out of the door with a canvas bag in his hands. Clad in a slicker, he moved toward a wagon that was approaching from the direction of the stable, driven by a trooper. Hammond could see six more troopers, on horseback, pull up to the front gate. He remembered then that this was mail day: Three times a week, Sergeant O'Malley made the trip into Apache Junction to deliver and pick up army mail coming in by stagecoach, and these days he was always accompanied by a mounted escort.

O'Malley climbed aboard the wagon and said something to the man with the reins, and the vehicle started to move. Catching sight then of Hammond standing on the porch of the officers' quarters, O'Malley waved. "Good morning, Lieutenant!" he called. "Anything I can get you in town?"

"Not today, thanks," Hammond replied. He watched as the wagon moved toward the gate, and just then a thought struck him. Now that he and Anita were formally betrothed, he wanted to buy her a set of rings. The general store in Apache Junction had catalogues from fancy jewelry emporiums back east, and he could ask the sergeant to pick up a catalogue for him.

He was about to call out to O'Malley when the wagon turned left, disappearing around the end of the row of buildings fronting the parade ground. Apparently the sergeant had to go to one of the supply buildings at the rear before departing for town. Not wanting to miss him, Hammond darted out into the rain and followed.

He caught up to the wagon as it was parked in front of the first supply building, where a trooper was handing O'Malley a package.

Hammond told O'Malley what he wanted, and after the sergeant assured him he would obtain the desired catalogue, the wagon headed for the gate.

Hammond was getting wet, so he took the shortest route to the colonel's office. Rounding the supply building, he was once again approaching the colonel's office from behind when he saw LuAnn Marlowe again. The beautiful blonde was saying something to Ballard, who stood at his back door; then she hurried away.

Hammond quickly backtracked around the corner of the supply building, so that he was out of her line of sight. Standing still for a moment, he felt as if a hot iron had been plunged into his heart. He had given the colonel the benefit of the doubt, but this repetition of yesterday's incident seemed to him to be open to only one interpretation.

Deeply disturbed, he made his way around to the front of the colonel's office and entered. As before, Corporal Sam Graves was not at his desk. Hammond moved to the inner door, knocked, and entered at the colonel's request.

Ballard looked him up and down and said, "Don't you own a slicker?"

"Oh, yes, sir," the lieutenant said, forcing a grin. "The rain is light, and I hadn't planned on being out in it long—but I had to catch Sergeant O'Malley before the wagon pulled out of the gate. I thought of something I wanted him to pick up for me in town."

Ballard nodded, told the lieutenant to sit down, and then sat down himself. "Well, Greg," he said in a cheerful, expansive tone, "how'd you sleep last night? Better than the night before, I hope."

"Not much, sir. You know, it isn't every day a man gets engaged."

"That's for sure," chuckled Ballard. Leaning forward, he put his elbows on the desk. "I wish you the very best, Greg. I hope you and my Anita can have as good a marriage as her mother and I have."

Hammond shifted uncomfortably in his chair. "Yes, sir," he said, trying to cover his feelings.

"Well," continued Ballard, "I want to hear all about the Apache attacks. Later this morning, I'm afraid you'll have to repeat the details slowly for Corporal Graves, so he can write them down. You know how the army is— always insists on explicit records, and the corporal's good with that sort of paperwork."

"I understand, sir," nodded Hammond.

He told the colonel as much as he could about the Apache attacks. At first he had planned to mention having to whip Lieutenant Radcliffe in order to keep him from killing the wounded Apache prisoner, but then he decided to leave that part out. Radcliffe would tell about it for sure, and Hammond preferred to let him display with his own words his ignorance of army procedure. If it earned him a dressing-down from the colonel, it would serve him right—and it might just teach him the discipline he needed to turn him into a leader of men.

"All right, that's fine," the colonel said when Hammond had finished. "Now, is there anything else you'd like to add, strictly *off* the record? That's the real reason I asked you to come here early this morning—to give you the chance to speak without your remarks being recorded."

Once again Hammond was tempted to describe the fight with Radcliffe, but he maintained his silence.

"No, sir, nothing to add."

"All right, then," the colonel replied, leaning back in his chair. "Is there anything else on your mind? Please speak freely. You know, with Captain Marlowe dead and Captain Oatman in the Apaches' hands, you're my senior officer at the moment. I'm relying on you."

Lieutenant Hammond gulped. The scenes with LuAnn leaped to the forefront of his mind—they were all he could think about. But he could not—must not—say anything to the colonel about them, and he had to work hard to keep his concern from being visible on his face.

"Nothing to report, sir," he said as blandly as he could. "Everything's fine. I think the men will all feel better now that the exchange of prisoners has been arranged."

"Good, good," the colonel replied. "That's all, then. Be here at eleven, to give your report to the corporal."

Hammond rose and turned to go.

"Oh, and Greg?" The colonel's voice stopped him, and Hammond turned back.

"Yes, sir?"

"Welcome to the family."

Hammond left the office, still feeling uneasy over his interview with the colonel and what he had seen for two mornings in a row. Why would a man with a lovely wife and two children who loved him dearly do such a thing? Did this explain why Mrs. Marlowe was able to stay at the fort? After all, it was no secret that Ballard had persuaded Lawrence Yarrow to give her a job. And everyone knew it was against army policy to permit the widow of a dead officer to remain for long in the officers' quarters. No one at Fort McDowell had thought anything about it, though. They all looked on it as an act of compassion on the colonel's part. *Was* it compassion? Or was it something else?

Hammond went to the guardhouse to tell Simino that the exchange of prisoners would be made that afternoon at three, and Simino was pleased to know he would be going home.

The rain stopped around nine o'clock. The clouds broke up within the next hour, and the sun was shining brightly when Hammond crossed the parade ground toward the colonel's office a few minutes before eleven o'clock.

It was just before noon when Corporal Sam Graves took down the last of Hammond's formal report. The colonel stepped into the outer office at that moment and, satisfied that the report was complete, asked the lieutenant to join him for lunch.

They were about to leave when Hammond glanced through the window and saw Sergeant O'Malley and the trooper pulling up in front of the office in the mail wagon. The trooper stepped from the wagon and carried a canvas sack to the mail office, while the sergeant made a beeline for the colonel's door. As he burst in, it was evident that he was upset.

"What's the matter, Sergeant?" Ballard asked.

O'Malley's glance darted to Hammond and then back to Ballard. "Chago!" he growled, as if the word burned his tongue to say it.

"Now what?" interjected Hammond.

"That animal and his Apaches attacked the Florence stage on its way into Apache Junction this mornin'. They killed everybody on board except an eight-year-old boy."

Hammond's eyes sparked with anger, and tight lines formed around his mouth. "That demonic excuse for a human being! It'd be a pleasure to squeeze the life out of him an inch at a time!"

"They're sure it was Chago?" queried Ballard.

"Yes, sir. When the boy was found, he kept cryin' and talkin' 'bout the 'mean-lookin' Indian in the red vest.' "

The colonel swore. "That's proof enough."

"I wonder why Chago and his bunch didn't kill the boy?" said Hammond.

"Can't say for sure, sir," replied O'Malley. "But the boy said the savages looted the stage before killin' the passengers. God, it must have been awful. The passengers probably knew what was comin'! Anyhow, his ma was with him—her name was on the company's passenger list. Maybe she found a way to hide him while the Apaches were busy with their lootin'. Boy was too broken up to say much, I'm told, so I'm just guessin'."

"Your guess is probably right. She must have been a courageous woman," Hammond sighed. He moved over to the open door and looked outside. He felt his anger rising, his face flushing, and his throat constricting, and he muttered oaths against Chago and his band.

Behind him, O'Malley said, "Only one good thing about this, sir."

"What's that?" asked Ballard.

"When the Apaches went through the stage, they didn't touch the mail. At least we got all of our mail."

"Well, that's something at least," commented Ballard, "though it doesn't count for much against all those lives lost."

Hammond brought his rage under control and turned back into the office. In a solemn tone he said, "Colonel, since Amanzus is apparently not going to deal with Chago, it looks like we will have to."

Ballard's features turned gray. "You're right, Lieutenant," he said grimly. "We can't let this go on. Chago must be stopped. But first we must keep our bargain with Amanzus, as we promised."

At three o'clock, as Lieutenant Hammond and his fifty men drew within sight of the prearranged meeting place, they could see the Apaches coming toward it from the opposite direction.

Simino rode an army bay between Hammond and Sergeant Chuck Foster. When they were within a hundred feet of the spring, he looked at Hammond and said, "Once again my thanks for saving my life, Lieutenant Greg Hammond."

Hammond smiled faintly and replied, "There is one wish I have concerning you, Simino."

"What is it?"

"I hope you never ride with Chago again on his murderous raids."

The Apache swallowed hard but did not comment.

Drawing up to the spring, Hammond carefully noted the boulders that marked the area. There were more than he remembered, but none was more than five feet high, and they were spread out.

The Indians drew up only seconds after the men in blue had pulled in and stopped. Hammond bit down on his lower lip when he saw Captain Hal Oatman on the back of a pinto, riding between Nachee and another warrior.

He looked gaunt and sick. His boots were gone, his shirt was ripped nearly to shreds, and his injured leg was bare except for a filthy bandage covering the wound.

Hammond glanced at Sergeant Foster, and the outrage on the sergeant's face mirrored his own.

Gazing at Nachee, Hammond thought how much he looked like his brother, and for an instant he almost wanted to strangle the Indian just because he resembled Chago so closely.

While the other troopers remained in their saddles, observing the Apaches warily, Greg Hammond and Chuck Foster dismounted. Stepping beside the bay that held Simino, Hammond looked up at him. "All right, Simino, you can get down."

The son of Amanzus, his right arm in a sling, had his wrists bound with thin rope. He extended them toward Hammond, who quickly untied the knots, and Simino, with a slight smile at the lieutenant, slid from his mount and walked toward his people.

The Apaches stayed on their horses as Nachee addressed Hammond, his eyes cold. "You may take your captain."

As Nachee spoke, Simino was just coming abreast of Captain Oatman's pinto. He stopped and was reaching up with his left arm to help the sick man down when Nachee spoke harshly. "Simino! Let the white-eyes lieutenant take care of this man!"

Glancing over at Nachee coldly, Simino eased the captain off the pinto with the strength of his left arm. Hal Oatman's eyes were half closed and his head bobbed listlessly as he came off the horse.

Hammond approached, with Sergeant Foster close behind. "I'll take him, Simino," the lieutenant said.

The Apache nodded. "White man has suffered much. Simino would carry him to horse if he had use of both arms."

The captain's mouth opened, weakly choking out the word, "Water."

Hammond picked up the captain in his arms and carried him as if he were a small child. "Sergeant," he directed, "bring a canteen." Then he spoke to Simino. "Thank you."

Simino nodded silently and stood watching as the lieutenant carried Oatman to the riderless bay, where Chuck Foster gave him a few sips of water.

"Captain, are you going to be able to stay on a horse?" Hammond asked.

"I . . . I think so," Oatman gasped. "If . . . if I could have some more water."

Sergeant Foster gave him another drink, and then Hammond and he hoisted the captain into the saddle.

Simino turned and walked toward his fellow warriors, many of whom gave him a warm greeting. He had some difficulty mounting the pinto using only his good arm; after he was finally settled on the animal's back, Nachee gave the command and the fifty Apache warriors rode away with Simino in their midst.

Hammond and Foster took a few more minutes to care for the wounded, dehydrated captain, then closed the canteen and mounted up. They placed Oatman's horse between them and prepared to move out.

Hammond leaned close and said, "Captain, are you sure you can ride by yourself? I could mount up behind you, you know—"

Already somewhat revived by the water, Oatman shook his head. "I'm fine, Greg. Let's head for home."

Hammond chuckled and said, "You're one tough hombre, Captain." Then he raised his arm and shouted to the men behind him, "Forward, ho!"

As he spoke, the crack of a rifle split the hot afternoon air. A bullet tore into the middle of Hal Oatman's back, and he grunted and fell from his horse.

Greg Hammond whipped around in time to see the red-vested Chago darting away amid some boulders off to the right, headed toward a pinto that was visible in a ravine. Chuck Foster swore as he spotted him, too.

Chago was on the pinto's back and riding away before the stunned men in blue could react. Hammond saw him look back and raise his rifle in a sign of victory, shaking the weapon to show his defiance.

Hammond leaped from his saddle to check on Oatman, with Chuck Foster right behind him. One look told both men that Oatman was dead. Hammond swore violently as he looked in the direction Chago had taken. "You snake!" he roared. "Your day is coming! I'll kill you myself!"

As the lieutenant stood up, one of the troopers said, "Let's go after him, Lieutenant!" The rest of the men spoke up in agreement.

Hammond shook his head. "That rabid wolf is with his pack now, and we'd be signing our own death warrants to go after them. We couldn't catch up to them till they were near enough their village to get reinforcements." He looked down at the captain and sighed. "Let's take Captain Oatman home. At least we can give him a decent burial."

The captain was laid to rest with full military honors, and later that same day Hammond wrote to the Oatman family back east. Colonel Ballard wrote to the family officially as commandant, but Hammond wanted to send his own words of consolation—for he had served under the captain and had learned much from him.

In the period after the funeral a kind of torpor fell over the fort, as the men awaited the colonel's next move. Something had to be done about Chago, but the colonel seemed disinclined to move hastily, probably because he knew that the Apache braves outnumbered any force he could put into the field. Though Hammond chafed at the inactivity, he knew that the colonel's position was not unreasonable.

Two days passed. On the third day, as Lieutenant Hammond left the mess hall after his midday meal and was crossing the sun-drenched parade ground toward the sutler's store, he noticed Colonel Ballard heading for the infirmary. Hammond slowed his pace and glanced over his shoulder covertly, watching Ballard enter the infirmary, and he wondered if the colonel was finally going to hear Bill Radcliffe's version of the Apache incidents.

Hammond entered the sutler's store and found it hot and stuffy. LuAnn Marlowe was behind the counter, running a feather duster over articles on the shelves behind her. There were no other customers in the store.

Turning around at the sound of his entrance, LuAnn flashed him a beguiling smile. "Good afternoon, Lieutenant. Pretty hot for spring, isn't it?"

Recalling her early-morning departures from the colonel's office, Hammond felt on edge in her presence. He had an urge to tell LuAnn what he thought of her, but he repressed it; after all, there still might be some legitimate explanation for what he had seen. Certainly both Mrs. Marlowe and the captain were innocent until proven guilty. He greeted her as casually as he could. "Yes, ma'am. It's real hot, and it may mean we're going to have a blistering summer."

"Is there anything you need today?" she asked.

"Just some shaving soap, ma'am," he said, pointing to the desired item on the shelf behind her.

LuAnn reached for the soap and set it on the counter. Hammond gave her a silver dollar, and as she was counting out the change, he remarked, "I was real sorry about Captain Dan, ma'am. I know you must miss him terribly."

As soon as the words were out of his mouth, Hammond felt a pang of remorse. If LuAnn *did* miss her husband, his comment could be deemed insensitive, perhaps opening wounds that were barely healed. But her reaction was calm as she said, "I miss him more than I could ever tell you, Lieutenant."

Seeing that she did not look particularly mournful, he decided to press her. "I know it must be lonely for you."

"Well," she sighed, "that's true. . . . I do get lonely at times. But I have my work here in the store. I just stay as busy as I can."

Greg nodded. "I'm sure that's the best thing to do."

Hammond was turning away when LuAnn inquired, "Lieutenant, what's this I hear about you and Anita getting engaged?"

Hammond's brow puckered, and he stared at LuAnn. He and Anita had decided to keep their engagement secret for the time being, until after the shock and grief over the recent killings had subsided. Her parents had strongly supported the decision to make no formal announcement of the engagement for several weeks.

"Where did you hear that news, ma'am?" Hammond countered.

LuAnn looked down quickly. "Oh . . . uh . . . let's see . . . I'm not sure. I . . . I think I overheard some of the men talking. Yes, that's what it was. I just happened to overhear their conversation while I was walking across the compound."

The familiar sick feeling crept into Hammond's stomach again. Only one person could have told her about the engagement: For some reason the colonel had seen fit to share the secret with her. Hammond had tried hard to believe that Ballard and LuAnn were not romantically involved, but the colonel's willingness to divulge a family confidence to her left him with little hope that his suspicions about them were unfounded. He wished now he had never seen the Marlowe woman emerging from the colonel's office.

Picking up the soap and turning to leave, Hammond said crustily over his shoulder, "We were trying to keep it a secret until we make a formal announcement."

"Oh," she said quickly, "please don't be upset with me. Of course I won't say anything to anyone about it."

Greg said no more but strode angrily out of the store. Returning to the brilliant sunlight, the lieutenant turned in the direction of his quarters. Then he saw the mail wagon was parked in front of the post office; Sergeant Francis O'Malley had apparently just returned from Apache Junction.

Hammond was about halfway across the parade ground when O'Malley emerged from the mail office waving something in his hand. "Lieutenant!" he called, stepping off the porch. "Here's your catalogue!"

The two men drew together and O'Malley apologized for having forgotten it the other day in the excitement of the attack on the stage. "And I'm afraid there's more bad news, sir," the sergeant added as Hammond took the catalogue.

"What's that?"

"The Florence stage was attacked by Chago and his bunch again this mornin'. Killed *everybody* on board this time. A rancher who was passin' hid in some brush nearby and saw it happen, and he reported to the stage-line agent that the leader of the hostiles was wearin' a red vest. This time Chago found gold on the stage."

Hammond's face went white, then red. There was a hard edge to his voice as he said, "We can't wait any longer to move on that dirty beast. We've got to move, and fast. We know Chago's men outnumber us, so we're going to have to figure out something that gets around that."

"I agree, sir," said O'Malley. "Things are only gonna get worse, 'specially now that Chago's found gold on that stage. He'll be hungry for more and lookin' for more and more stages to raid."

"You're right, Sergeant," Hammond nodded. "But even without the gold, that mad dog is going to go on killing until he's dead. He's just made that way."

"I guess so, sir." The sergeant saluted and started to walk away.

Suddenly a thought occurred to the lieutenant. "Sergeant?" he called. "Did you hear anything more about the boy—I mean the one who survived the raid the other day?"

Sergeant O'Malley stopped. "Yes, sir, as a matter of fact I did. Seems his mother was a widow. The stage company has the address of her parents in Houston, and they're bein' notified; meanwhile a family in town is takin' care of the boy. Most likely the company'll give him his fare back to his kinfolk and send someone along with him to see that he gets aboard the Southern Pacific's eastbound coach out of Florence. The Southern Pacific officials will be alerted that he's coming. But none of that'll happen till after these killins' are over."

"Thanks, Sergeant. I'm glad someone's looking after the boy. He's been through a lot."

As Lieutenant Hammond went about his routine duties during the afternoon, his mind was at work on a plan to annihilate the Apache killer.

After finishing his evening meal in the mess hall, the determined lieutenant had his plan perfected. He decided to discuss it with Colonel Ballard right away. If the colonel approved of it and the necessary items were available, Chago would die, and soon.

Anita Ballard answered Hammond's knock. "Well, if it isn't the handsome, charming Lieutenant Gregory L. Hammond! I was hoping you would find time to come see me!" The beautiful redhead rushed into his arms, and they kissed.

"Darling, I wish I had time to spend with you this evening, but I need to talk to your father. Is he here?"

"No, he's over at his office. Said he had some important paperwork to do. Dear me, I hope your business won't keep you too long. . . ."

"I don't know, darling. Chago's attacked another stage. But I've got a plan that just may stop him."

Anita expressed her concern, and Hammond kissed her again before turning to stride across the parade ground.

As he entered the colonel's outer office, he was surprised to find the door to the inner office wide open. He glanced through it and then froze in his tracks, for he could see Colonel Ballard and LuAnn Marlowe locked in a passionate embrace.

They broke immediately, their eyes wide with surprise.

Hammond stared at them for a few seconds and then stepped backward, stammering, "Excuse me." Then he moved out quickly, shutting the outer door behind him.

He was burning with fury as he stepped onto the parade ground, in despair over the confirmation of all his suspicions. What the colonel and LuAnn were doing was wrong; they were endangering the happiness of too many people.

Walking briskly toward his quarters, the distraught lieutenant pondered what he should do. He was not even sure he had the right to do anything: He was not a member of the family yet, and even if he were, what could he do? To tell Esther, Anita, or Art about what he had seen would hurt them deeply, and to no purpose. He decided that above all he would not act hastily. Sighing, he realized that dealing with emotional and personal issues could be even tougher than making military decisions.

Back in the office, LuAnn Marlowe watched the door shut behind Greg Hammond.

"That meddlesome lieutenant!" she cried, exasperated. "Does he always barge in when he's not wanted?" She dug her fingernails into Ballard's shirtsleeves and said, "Well, we're no longer a secret now, darling. The entire fort will know about us for sure! You'd best tell Esther right now that you want a divorce, and we'll get this whole thing over with! We've discussed this before, and you know it's the only thing to do."

Ballard shook his head. "I don't think so."

"What do you mean? The man just saw us! He's engaged to your daughter! Do you honestly think—?"

"That's just the point," Ballard said, cutting across her words. "He's engaged to my daughter. He'll want to spare Anita and the family from being hurt, so I don't think he'll say a word. Besides, LuAnn, I've told you before that everything is down the drain if I divorce Esther. My career will be finished. No, things'll just have to remain as they are."

Thwarted again in her deepest wishes, LuAnn came back to a thought she had often had before: If Esther met with some accident . . . if somehow, something happened . . . Yes, that was the only way. LuAnn was now more determined than ever to remove the one person who stood in the way of her becoming the wife of Fort McDowell's commandant.

Straightening her hair and kissing the colonel, she bade him good night and left as usual by the back door.

Chapter Eleven

Lieutenant Greg Hammond tossed and turned sleeplessly throughout the night. Though tormented about what to do with his knowledge of the colonel's affair with LuAnn Marlowe, he also had his mind on his plan to kill Chago.

Finally rising just before dawn, he wearily shaved and dressed in the dark, and then went to the stable to saddle his horse.

The guards in the tower beside the main gate leaned over the rail and squinted at the dark figure on the bay horse. One of them called, "Is that you, Lieutenant Hammond?"

"Yes," replied Hammond. "I want you to do me a favor."

"Certainly, sir."

"I've got business in Apache Junction early this morning. I tried to see the commandant last night, but he was busy. Will you get a message to him for me? Tell him that I've gone to town on an errand that involves our problem with Chago. I'll be back by noon and will explain it to him then."

"Will do, sir," said the guard.

Bright yellow sunbeams crept across the desert from

the eastern horizon, throwing lengthy shadows over the town of Apache Junction as Hammond rode up to the stage company's office and slid from his saddle. The office would not be open for another forty minutes, but Hammond knew that the agent, Wally Becker, lived in the apartment above. Seeing that a window on the second floor was open, he called out Becker's name.

Presently the middle-aged man stuck his lathered face out the window and said, "Lieutenant! Surprised to see you here at this hour. Somethin' I can do for you?"

"I know you're not open yet, but I need to see you now."

"If it has anythin' to do with ridin' a stage, you can forget it. The company wired me last night. They've canceled all the runs between Apache Junction and Florence 'cause of them bloodthirsty Apaches attackin' the stages and killin' everybody. In fact, they've stopped runs from the other direction, too, so there's nothin' movin' between here and Phoenix. They won't be runnin' stages here till after you soldier boys get the redskins under control."

"I think that's wise," replied Hammond. "In fact, that's exactly what I'm here about. We're about to put a stop to the killings, and I need your help."

"In that case, I'll be right down to let you in," grinned Becker.

Moments later Hammond was seated in the upstairs apartment, watching the agent as he finished shaving in front of a mirror.

"Go ahead and talk, Lieutenant," he said, scraping at his whiskers.

"You've had some of your stagecoaches shot up pretty badly," said Hammond. "Are any of them here in town?"

"Couple of 'em," responded the agent. "One of 'em's the stage your colonel's family was on. Got a man repairin' 'em in his barn at the east edge of town."

"Do you suppose the California & Arizona Stage Company would mind losing one of its coaches if it meant putting a stop to Chago?"

Becker paused, soap dripping from his chin. Smiling, he said, "I think the top brass would agree it was worth it."

"Are you willing to take a chance on that, or will I have to wait while you go through all kinds of red tape to get permission?"

"I'll take the chance. What have you got in mind?"

Becker went back to his shaving as Hammond explained. "About a month ago I heard that a team of geologists from back east was digging in a rocky area about twenty miles east of here. I was told they'd be there for several weeks. Do you know if they're still there?"

"They sure are. But what have they got to do with Chago?"

"I was also told they were using nitroglycerin to blow their way into some difficult rock enclosures."

"That's right. Jack Post over at the gun shop is supplyin' 'em with it. I've heard that nitro is pretty potent stuff. You know much about it?"

"A little. I've seen it used a time or two. They take glycerin, which by itself is a harmless liquid, and mix it with two kinds of acid—sulfuric and nitric."

"I see," said Becker, laying down his straight-edge razor and bending over a washbasin to splash water on his face.

"It's the blend of the acids with the glycerin that makes it so potent. Once the mixture is complete, all it takes is the slightest jarring to make it explode."

Becker raised a towel to his face and nodded.

"So what they do," proceeded Hammond, "is add only one of the acids to the glycerin until they're ready to use the stuff. Usually they put in the sulfuric first, because the nitric acid contains nitrogen, which is a gas."

"Yeah."

"Get it all together and disturb it just slightly, and . . . *boom!*"

Dabbing at his freshly shaven face with the towel, the

agent asked, "So you're gonna use nitroglycerin on Chago. How you gonna do it?"

"I want to plant a sufficient amount of it in one of the damaged coaches and leave it somewhere on the road between here and Florence, where Chago usually strikes. The rack can be loaded with boxes that look as if they hold something valuable. After my men and I park the coach on the side of the road, we'll remove a wheel, making it look as if the coach broke down and the crew and passengers walked the horses into town. I'll have some men actually take the team from the stage and walk it away, to leave convincing tracks. We'll do it at night, and when the Apaches come along during the day, they'll figure what must have happened. Their curiosity—and their greed—will make them climb on the stage and inspect the boxes."

Becker was now putting on his shirt. "I can see how this will work real good, since Chago doesn't know the runs have been canceled. But how were you figurin' to do it if the coaches were still runnin'?"

"It would have been a matter of your wiring the head office and persuading them to cancel one run. Then I would have replaced that one coach with the broken-down stage."

"I see," nodded the agent. "All right, so you're a smart fella. Now let's say Chago and his boys take your bait. How do you set off the nitro, which I assume is in the boxes?"

"I'll be hiding nearby with a few of my men. When Chago and his warriors are in the most vulnerable position, I will personally fire a rifle bullet into the nitro and blow them to their happy hunting ground."

A broad smile worked its way across the agent's face. "Sounds good to me. When do you want to do it?"

"There ordinarily would be a stage due tomorrow, wouldn't there?"

"Yes."

"What time would it be coming?"

"Well, actually we'd been staggerin' the times of the runs, hopin' to get 'em past the Apaches, but they must have had scouts out. No matter what times we tried, Chago got there to attack the stages."

Hammond scratched his head. "Well, for sure they won't have any scouts out at night. When they spot the stage, they may even think you tried a night run to fool them. The main thing is to get them to move in close to the coach."

"Lieutenant," laughed Becker, "you're a genius. If you get Chago, the company'll probably pin a medal on you. I guess you'll want the coach tonight?"

"Yes. I'm going to the gun shop now to see if your friend Jack Post can supply me with some nitro."

"Shouldn't be any problem," commented the agent. "He's still supplyin' it for those university boys. Saw 'em over there just yesterday."

Hammond thanked Becker for his cooperation and told him that he and his men would be back after dark. He then went to the gun shop, where he found Jack Post very willing to supply the nitroglycerin—so willing, in fact, that he donated it for the cause. Hammond explained that he wanted enough to kill anyone within a hundred feet of the coach when the nitro exploded. Post told him he would prepare a sufficient amount and even offered to go along to complete the mixture at the site himself, so as not to endanger any of the soldiers.

Hammond expressed his gratitude for Post's help, saying he would be back after dark.

Hammond passed through the main gate of Fort McDowell just before noon. Looking up at the guard in the tower, he said, "Did you get my message to Colonel Ballard?"

"Sure did, sir," came the answer.

Hammond thanked him and moments later stepped into the colonel's outer office. Corporal Marvin

Graves was at his desk, poring over a ledger book. Looking up, he said, "Hello, Lieutenant. Colonel Ballard is over at the sutler's store at the moment. He said to tell you he'd be right back in case you got here before he returned."

Hammond frowned at the news. *Maybe Yarrow's out of the store, and the colonel and LuAnn are discussing what I'm going to do,* he thought.

"You really think he'll be back soon?" he asked the corporal. "I can always come back at another time."

"Shouldn't be long, sir," replied Graves. "It might be best if you stick close, 'cause the colonel seemed quite interested to know if you have something planned for Chago."

Greg heard someone greet the colonel outside and, turning to see Ballard coming toward the office, wondered how their first meeting since the incident last night would be.

Ballard stepped up on the porch and paused momentarily when he observed Hammond standing inside the outer office. He did not meet Hammond's eyes as he moved through the door and said, "Looks like another hot spring day, eh, Lieutenant?" Without breaking stride, he moved into the inner office, speaking over his shoulder and telling Hammond to come in.

Hammond passed through the second door and moved toward the desk. Ballard stepped behind it with brisk movements, sat down, and then motioned toward the door and said, "Close it, will you, Lieutenant?"

Hammond obeyed and then drew up to the desk. Still evasive with his eyes, Ballard looked down at the desktop and said, "Sit down."

Greg eased into the chair and gazed at the colonel, saying nothing.

"Well," said Ballard without looking up, "you have something to tell me? Could it be a plan to rid us of that red-vested pest?"

Greg wanted to tell him that he had come to the

office last night to discuss the matter with him, but he thought better of it. Adjusting himself to a more comfortable position in the chair, he replied, "Yes, sir."

The colonel's eyes rose and met Hammond's, and he listened intently as the lieutenant took him step by step through the plan he had set in motion for that very night.

When he was finished, the colonel gave him a pleased look. "I admire your initiative." Then he looked thoughtful. "Of course you'll have to shoot from a pretty good distance to ensure the safety of your men and yourself. But one thing's for sure: You're a crack shot, and it should be no problem for you to hit one of those boxes."

"I won't miss, sir," replied Hammond. "Do you want to assign me the men for this duty, or should I pick them myself?"

"This is your show," came the quick answer. "You pick the men you want."

"Very well, sir," Hammond said, rising to his feet. "I'll get right on it. There's a lot to do."

Keeping his seat, Ballard rushed to say, "You have a good head on your shoulders, Greg. This stratagem of yours shows some very sharp thinking. You'll go far in the army. In fact I . . . uh . . . I don't want to get myself out on a limb here, but maybe it would be good for you to know about something I'm doing. You're aware that with the deaths of Marlowe and Oatman, this fort is in need of a couple more captains. I've wired Washington about this, but I've requested only *one* new captain and *one* new lieutenant. That is, I . . . recommended that they promote you to be my second captain and send me a new lieutenant to fill the slot you now hold. What do you think of that?"

In the light of recent events, this sounded to Hammond like a bribe. The colonel was trying to buy his silence. He felt his chest tighten. Looking the colonel squarely in the eye, he asked, "When did you do this, sir?"

"Just this morning," replied Ballard, standing up behind the desk and moving slowly around it.

Hammond nodded woodenly and then said with a dull voice, "Just this morning. I see."

Ballard took a deep breath and rubbed a hand over his brow. He paused for a long moment before speaking again. "Now, Greg," he said with a slight tremor in his voice, "you're a fine officer, fully deserving of the promotion I've asked for. I'd have put through a request sooner, but as I think you can understand, things have been pretty busy around here."

Hammond felt his face heat up. "Yes, sir."

"What with Chago and all, I mean," the colonel added quickly.

"Yes, sir." Hammond could feel his face flushing even more.

The colonel looked down, took another long breath, and then gazed directly at Hammond. "As I said the other day, Greg, I'm relying on you. I know I can trust you. You've got to understand that a commandant has a great many responsibilities, some of them not strictly . . . military in nature. What I mean is . . . well, I wouldn't want you to draw any . . . inappropriate inferences from what you may have seen here last night."

"I have perfect eyesight, sir. I saw what I saw."

"What I'm saying, son," Ballard said, his voice rising, "is that what may have looked to you like . . . an indiscretion was actually something quite different. You must believe that."

"I would like to, sir," came Hammond's dry reply.

"What happened, Greg, was that Mrs. Marlowe was having one of her blue spells that she says she has been experiencing since Dan was killed. She was out walking, eating her heart out with grief and loneliness. She saw the light burning in my office and stepped in to talk. She just needed a listening ear. You know how that is."

"Yes, sir."

"Well, she poured out her heart to me, and when I tried to comfort her, she threw herself into my arms. I guess she needed the support that only a man can provide. Women arc unpredictable, and . . . well, she really caught me off guard. You just happened to come through the door at that very moment."

Hammond wished that what he was being told were the truth, but he knew better. Ballard had been kissing LuAnn as passionately as she had kissed him. He decided to test Ballard. "May I ask you this, sir? Has Mrs. Marlowe done this before? I mean, has she ever come to see you before last night, when she's depressed or lonely?"

The colonel was already shaking his head before Greg had finished asking his question. "No, certainly not, Greg," he said. "Last night was the first time."

Convinced by this blatant lie that the colonel's affair with LuAnn was an indisputable fact, Hammond felt his heart sink. He decided to carry the matter no further at this point. Pretending to believe Ballard, he thanked him for the recommendation of a promotion, and as he rose to leave the office, he saw the colonel's face relax. Obviously the older man thought he had successfully established that all he had been doing the night before was comforting a grieving widow.

Hammond stepped out into the bright blast of sunlight and headed for the sutler's store, hoping to find LuAnn Marlowe.

The young widow needed to take a good look at what she was doing, he decided. Her affair with the colonel could cause a lot of damage, and maybe a face-to-face talk with her about the situation would encourage her to break off the relationship.

Hammond was nearing the store when he saw the door open and Anita Ballard emerge with a couple of packages in her hands. She saw Greg immediately and stepped off the porch in his direction, the sun highlighting her red hair as she approached.

"Hello, darling," Anita said as she reached him. "What have you been doing today?"

"Making plans for Chago," he replied, and then quickly changed the subject. "Oh! I meant to tell you . . . I had Sergeant O'Malley pick me up a catalogue from one of those jewelry outlets back east. We need to go through it and pick out your rings. I want to buy you an engagement ring, and I figure I might just as well get the wedding ring at the same time."

"Oh, Greg!" she exclaimed, dropping her packages and throwing her arms around him and kissing him. "That's wonderful!"

Hammond hugged her, but looked around nervously. "Honey," he said in a low tone, "we haven't announced our engagement yet. Maybe we'd better not be *too* public with our affections."

"You're right, darling," she said, easing back. "It's just that I'm so excited, and I'll be so proud to be wearing an engagement ring."

Looking down at her dreamily, Greg breathed, "I'm the one who will be proud. Anyway, I'm afraid I've got things to do now, so I'll come by your house later."

"See that you do, Lieutenant Hammond, and that's an order!" she said, winking at him. "And bring the catalogue when you come."

"Will do." He smiled and then moved toward the store.

As he entered the sutler's establishment, LuAnn Marlowe and Lawrence Yarrow were unpacking a large box of dry goods. Hammond could see LuAnn's face lose a bit of its color when she saw who had come in, and she seemed to grow even paler as he greeted Yarrow and then set his gaze on her.

"Mrs. Marlowe, would it be possible for me to talk to you for a few minutes?" Hammond said evenly.

"Well, I don't know," she replied, wiping her hands on an apron she wore. "Mr. Yarrow and I are quite busy—"

"Oh, that's all right, LuAnn," the sutler cut in. "No customers are here and we can unpack these things later. Go ahead and take a few minutes to talk to the lieutenant."

The lovely blonde led Hammond out the back door onto a porch. It was occupied mostly by stacks of empty boxes, but there were two old hardbacked chairs at one end. LuAnn and Hammond sat down, and she eyed him warily. When he didn't speak right away, she broke the silence. "I suppose this is about last night."

"Yes, ma'am," he nodded. "I see something happening here that I don't like. People are going to get hurt. Ordinarily I'd say that it's none of my business, but since you know that Anita and I are to be engaged, you can understand that I have a legitimate stake in this family's happiness."

The blond woman's features were rigid. "Have you spoken with the colonel about this?"

"Yes, ma'am, only moments ago."

"And what did he say?"

"He attributed the whole thing to the fact that you were lonely and grieving. Said you happened by the office, went in to talk, and what I saw was him consoling you while your emotions were running high."

"Well?"

"I pretended to believe him, but I know it's a lie."

"Oh," she said, her voice rising in pitch, "how do you know that?"

Looking her straight in the eye, he said, "Have there been other times when you've been alone with the colonel in his office?"

Recoiling slightly as if in shock, LuAnn said, "Why, of course not! It's as he told you, I just went in to talk and . . . well, my emotions got the better of me."

Fixing her with his dark brown eyes, Hammond said, "You are lying, Mrs. Marlowe."

As she opened her mouth to protest, he said levelly, "I have seen you coming out of the colonel's office myself . . . *twice* . . . in the last few days. From the *back* door. Both times at a few minutes before seven in the morning. Are you telling me you were seeking his 'consolation' on both those occasions?"

LuAnn took a deep breath and pulled herself erect, a look of defiance on her face. "All *right,* so we've been seeing each other. What of it?"

"I'll put it real plain, ma'am. I want you to break this thing off. Stay away from the colonel. Don't break up his home."

LuAnn stared at him, her features reddening. Hostility showed in her eyes, and her lips pulled into a thin line. Through her set teeth she hissed, "Who are you to tell me what to do, mister? If you think—"

"You know as well as I do that I have every right, as Anita's future husband," cut in Hammond. "I'm telling you, if you don't break off this relationship, I'll be forced to expose your affair. If you insist on breaking the hearts of Esther, Anita, and Art, I'll see that it's done immediately. I'll make sure you get caught in the backlash. You'll find I'm tough as nails if I have to be."

LuAnn said not a word, but stared at the lieutenant. She seemed to be pondering something, her mind almost distant. Then Hammond saw her features change, taking on a different aspect. Her expression softened; a look of defeat and resignation appeared on her face, and her shoulders drooped. It was as if something within her had broken, and she began to cry.

Hammond fidgeted uncomfortably in his chair. Women crying always disconcerted him, and he did not know how to react. He was on the point of saying something to ease the situation when she spoke.

"Oh, Lieutenant Hammond, what have I done?" she exlaimed, her lips trembling. "I've been so selfish in all of this! The colonel was right, in a way, when he said that he was consoling me. That's how it started. . . . After my husband's death, he was so gentle and considerate. I really did miss the captain, and the colonel was so . . . understanding. We never meant it to be more than that. It just happened. Surely you, as a sensitive and intelligent man, can grasp that. We only saw each other a few times. But

now, I . . . I realize now how very wrong we've been."
Touching his hand, she drew in a shuddering breath. "Can
you ever forgive me?"

Taken aback by her headlong confession of wrongdoing,
Greg withdrew his hand gently and stammered, "Ma'am, I
. . . appreciate your telling me this, and I guess I can see
how things might have developed. If you will promise me
it's over, I'll forgive you and drop it right here."

"Yes," she nodded, squeezing her eyelids tight, tears
spilling. "I'll talk to Phil—to the colonel right away. I'll
tell him we can't see each other anymore. Oh, I've been
so wrong!"

Hammond stood up, looked down at her, and said,
"Thank you, ma'am. You're doing the right thing." With
that, he stepped off the porch and disappeared around the
corner of the store.

LuAnn sat for a moment by herself. She had always
wanted to be an actress, and she had just played the role
of her life.

She knew when that young lieutenant came to her
that she had been trapped, and that Hammond, obviously
a rash and determined young man, had meant what he
said about exposing her. He was also dangerous because
he was very much in love and would do anything to
protect Anita and her family. The situation could become
very messy. And so she had bought time by feigning
repentance—acting very well, she thought, certainly well
enough to convince that meddlesome puppy of a lieutenant.
But in the long run she would win. She would get what
she wanted.

The whole episode only strengthened her resolve to
remove Esther Ballard somehow. That would have to wait,
of course, until the moment was right, since LuAnn could
not be implicated in any way. But in the meantime, she
realized, there were immediate steps she could take to get
even with that self-righteous Greg Hammond!

The beautiful blonde smiled to herself and then rose and went back into the store, where the sutler was still unpacking goods. "Mr. Yarrow," she said, "I need to see Colonel Ballard for just a few minutes. Would that be all right?"

"Certainly," he nodded.

As she crossed the parade ground, LuAnn found her anger over the lieutenant and the way in which he had trapped her growing stronger. She kept her feelings in check, however, as she stepped into the colonel's outer office, where she put on a pleasant smile and said in a calm voice, "Corporal Graves, is the colonel in his office?"

Rising, Graves said, "Yes, ma'am. I'll tell him you're here."

LuAnn waited impatiently while the corporal tapped on the door and announced her arrival. She heard Ballard tell Graves to bring her in, and moving in a casual manner, LuAnn passed through the door, smiled at Graves, and took a seat in front of the desk.

As soon as the corporal had closed the door, she sprang out of the chair with fire in her eyes and clutched Ballard's arm. She whispered frantically, "You've got to get rid of Greg Hammond! I don't care what it takes—get him out of here at all costs!"

That same day at the Apache village, the men were involved in a game that had been popular with the Indians for generations. It was played with a hoop three feet in diameter and a stick thirty to forty inches long. The object was to keep the hoop rolling for as long as possible; a player started his hoop with his hands, but thereafter could use only the stick to keep it moving.

Hours of leisure were devoted to this game, as the onlookers bet money or valuable articles on the outcome. On this particular day, an elimination tournament was in progress; gold stolen during the latest stagecoach raid had changed hands several times during the contest, and now it was in a pile to be claimed by the winner in the final round of the tournament. Two players were vying for the winner's spot: Chago and his brother, Nachee.

As the last round began, the crowd in the village, gathered in a large circle, shouted and clapped as the two brothers moved about adeptly, keeping their hoops erect.

The pressure mounted as time passed. The crowd tensed on several occasions, when one or the other brother nearly let his hoop fall. A half hour had passed when suddenly Chago's hoop bounced on a small stone, careened away from the tip of his stick, and dropped on its side. The villagers gave Nachee a wild cheer and applauded his victory.

When the crowd had settled down, Chago—who detested losing in any kind of contest—approached Nachee and said, "I would like one more opportunity to win the gold."

Nachee laughed. "But I am going to spend it, my brother! I have plans for it!"

Chago firmed his jaw and said, "I am your brother, Nachee. You should give me another chance to win it."

Nachee said, "What can you put up against the gold? I will not play you unless there is something of value I can win."

"I have the beautiful nickle-plated Remington rifle I stole from the driver of that last stagecoach. I will put it up against your gold."

Nachee shook his dark head. "I have a good rifle already. That is not satisfactory."

Chago swung a hand toward the corral. "I will put up my beautiful new pinto!"

Nachee shrugged. "I have a pinto already." Then a sly look captured his eyes. "But one thing I do not have, my brother. If you will put it up against the gold, I will play you one more round."

"What is that?" grunted Chago.

"Your red vest."

Chago looked down at the vest and touched it tenderly with his fingertips. It was well known that Chago prized this vest above all other possessions and would be most reluctant to part with it. Chago thought for a moment and then said, "All right. I can beat you. I will put up the vest against your gold."

The crowd watched intently as the round began. Chago was playing with a wicked grin on his face, obviously confident he could beat his brother this time.

The hot sun pounded down on the skillful contestants as the contest went on for over forty minutes. Both men had come close to dropping their hoops, but they were still in control when suddenly the two hoops collided. Nachee was able to keep his hoop going, but Chago's fell flat in the dust. Amid the whoops and applause Nachee smiled broadly, extending his hand toward his brother. Chago, his face grim, took off the vest and placed it in Nachee's hand. More cheering followed, and when the noise of the throng died down, Nachee put his arm around his brother's shoulder while holding the prized vest in the other hand.

"I will give you a chance to win the vest back, Chago," he smiled. "Next week!"

Chago smiled good-naturedly as the people laughed and Nachee put on the vest. "All right, my brother," Chago conceded. "You wear it for a few days; then I will win it back!"

Chapter Twelve

Chago and Nachee were consuming rabbit stew for breakfast early the next morning when two Apache scouts came riding into the village from the east. Drawing rein where the brothers sat, they slid from their pintos' backs.

Chago looked up. "Ah, Tana and Eskamon, you have sighted an approaching stagecoach already?"

At fourteen, Eskamon was still learning from the older Tana how to be a scout. Therefore it was Tana who spoke. "Something very strange, Chago," he said. "We have spotted a stagecoach, but it is standing on the side of the road."

Chago laid down the bowl of stew and stood up. "And what are the people doing?"

"We saw no people. Eskamon and I did not go too close, but we could tell that nobody was there, and even the horses were gone. I think they had trouble, for one of the wheels was off and leaning against the side of the stagecoach."

Nachee, proudly wearing the red vest he had won from Chago, rose to his feet. "The crafty whites have tried to sneak a stagecoach past us," he declared. "Can you see, my brother? They drove it at night in order to avoid our attack."

"Yes, of course," smiled Chago, letting the smile turn into a wicked sneer. "And it seems that it did not go as well as planned. I wonder if they were carrying more gold."

"Tell him about the boxes," spoke up Eskamon.

Nodding, Tana said, "We saw several on top of the coach. They looked sturdy and could hold something of value." Sneering now himself, he added, "They probably did not have any volunteers to remain behind and guard the boxes."

Chago laughed wickedly. "I do not blame them! If you were white-eyes, how would *you* like to face Apache warriors alone?"

Nachee and Eskamon both laughed, and Chago gave instructions to his brother. "Nachee, gather six warriors and let us ride quickly to see what we can find in the boxes." To Tana he remarked, "You will go with us and lead us to the stagecoach."

Eskamon stepped close to the rugged leader. "Chago, I would like to go along."

"No," Chago replied flatly. "You are too young, and it is possible we will meet up with soldier-coats coming to guard the coach. You will remain here."

At that moment, a lone rider came in from the north. Chago recognized him as Lamgo, a Jicarilla Apache from the northern mountains. When the rider drew up and dismounted from his sweaty horse, Chago saw a solemn look on his face.

"Lamgo," Chago said, raising his hand in greeting. "You have ridden hard, my friend, and you seem troubled."

"Yes, Chago," said Lamgo. "There is great discord among my people, and they have sent me to bring you back among us. Our chief, Ramino, is ill and has not long to live. A serious dispute is raging over who will become his successor."

"I am grieved to learn that Ramino is dying," Chago said, genuinely moved.

"Chago," Lamgo went on, "Since you were a mighty warrior among us, our people want you to come and settle the dispute, to prevent bloodshed. This is Ramino's own wish as well. All have agreed that whomever you select will be chief of our tribe. You *will* come?"

"Of course," nodded Chago gravely. "It is a duty I cannot refuse. Ramino was my friend when I was among your people, and on one occasion he saved my life." Chago turned to his brother. "Nachee, you take the six warriors and Tana and see what is in the boxes on top of the stagecoach. I must go with Lamgo."

Chago gave a quick explanation to Chief Amanzus about the problem among the Jicarillas, and Amanzus asked that his personal greetings be conveyed to Ramino, should Chago reach him in time. Then Chago gathered his weapons and provisions for the journey and rode out with Lamgo.

As Nachee, the six chosen warriors, and Tana were mounting up for the trip to the stagecoach, Eskamon approached Nachee and pleaded once more, "Please let me go with you. I would like to see what is in the boxes."

"No, Chago is right," Nachee told him. "You are too young. As a scout you were able to observe the coach from a safe distance, but we shall have to get much closer to it, and if soldier-coats should come, they will attack. I cannot put you in such danger."

Crestfallen, Eskamon stood in the center of the village and watched the eight warriors gallop away to the east. After waiting about fifteen minutes, he casually moved to his pinto, swung up on its back, and rode out. No one noticed him going in the same direction Nachee had taken earlier.

Lieutenant Greg Hammond lay on his stomach atop a towering rock a little over a hundred yards from the spot where the stagecoach had been set up. In his hands was a long-barreled, breech-loading .44-caliber Winchester rifle, his own personal weapon. He had proven himself accurate with it at eight hundred yards, so hitting the boxes in the rack of the stagecoach from this distance would be quite easy.

At the base of the rock, thirty feet below, were ten other men in blue, as a safety measure in case more Apaches happened to be in the area when Chago and his bunch gathered around the coach.

As he waited Hammond reflected with satisfaction that everything had gone according to plan so far. During the night men from the fort had set up the stagecoach and then walked the team away from it toward town, to leave prints that would make the breakdown appear to be authentic. Jack Post had prepared the nitro, and at Hammond's request he had placed enough of the deadly chemical in the boxes to kill anyone within a hundred feet of the coach.

It was nearly eight o'clock when from his high position Hammond saw Apaches riding across the desert toward the abandoned stagecoach. They were mounted on fine-looking pintos, and for a moment the lieutenant felt something akin to regret. He loved animals and admired the spirited steeds the Indians rode; he hated having to kill them. But it could not be helped: Chago had to be stopped before more people were killed, and the pintos would have to be sacrificed.

The Indians drew closer, and Hammond smiled to himself when he saw the sun shining on the bright red vest worn by the lead rider. Leaning over the edge of the rock, he called down, "Here they come, men! Keep out of sight!"

"Don't miss, Lieutenant!" yelled Sergeant Chuck Foster.

"He won't miss, Sergeant!" snapped one of the men gruffly.

Foster chuckled, "I know it, soldier. I was just kiddin'."

"How many are there, Lieutenant?" asked one of the other men.

"I count eight," replied Hammond. "Chago and seven of his buddies. One of them's without a rifle—he may be a scout. Now quiet down. They're getting close."

The soldiers fell silent, and Greg Hammond pulled his head down as far as he could and still see the Apaches riding up to the stagecoach. Positioning his rifle, he pulled back the hammer and locked it in place. He sighted down the barrel, flexing his hand eagerly next to the trigger guard. "Go ahead, boys," he said in a low tone. "Climb up there and take a good look in those boxes. Especially you, Chago. Get nice and close."

Down on the ground the eight Indians drew up to the disabled Concord coach and dismounted. Hammond saw the red-vested leader examine the wheel and then the prints leading away from the coach, pointing them out to the others, who nodded. The ruse was working.

The red-vested commander directed three braves to climb up and open the boxes, while two more moved inside the coach. The two remaining Indians went to the rear boot of the coach, where they began unbuckling the leather straps that held the lid down. Seconds later the first three Apaches were on top of the coach, trying to open the boxes. At this instant the leader turned his back on the coach, taking a few steps away from it and surveying the landscape, doubtless to make sure that no whites were approaching.

Sighting down the rifle, Greg Hammond picked a box between two of the Apaches on the coach roof. Just before he squeezed the trigger, he saw the dark-skinned man in the vest turn toward him. From that distance, Hammond could not make out his features. "Good-bye, Chago," he breathed.

The rifle bucked in Hammond's hands, sending its roar across the dry land, but the sound was drowned out by the deafening thunder of exploding nitroglycerin. Shock waves rocked the desert floor as eight Apaches and eight pintos were blown to bits amid a sheet of fire and billows of smoke.

The lieutenant came down from his perch and rejoined his men. One or two of the soldiers started to move forward, but Hammond restrained them. They needed to wait for a minute or two, he explained, to be sure that no further explosions occurred. It was almost certain that all the nitro had blown at once, but Hammond was taking no chances.

Finally the lieutenant moved toward the coach, the soldiers following. One or two of them were still rubbing their ears after the deafening explosion.

The scene before them was one of utter devastation. Shattered bits of the stagecoach were strewn everywhere, but what was worse to behold were the fragments of men and animals. One private turned away, sick to his stomach, and even Sergeant Foster, hardened to such sights, looked pale.

Hammond spotted the upper half of a body with tattered fragments of a red vest clinging to it, and steeling himself, he approached to get a closer look. Two or three of the men followed.

They found what was left of the upper torso, with the face pointed skyward. Because the leader's back had been to the stagecoach when the nitro exploded, his face was still intact. Greg Hammond's eyes bulged as he focused on the features of the face. He gasped as if he had been hit in the midsection with a battering ram, and there were murmurs and groans among the men when they saw that the dead Apache in the red vest was not Chago but his brother, Nachee.

Sergeant Foster swore and ran his gaze over the area, trying to see if Chago could have been there.

Greg Hammond, his voice heavy with disappointment, said, "It's no use, Sergeant. Chago's not among them. The one in the red vest was giving orders to the others." Pausing, he removed his hat, ran his fingers through his hair, and lamented, "The dirty beast is still alive. Why wasn't he leading them, and why was Nachee wearing Chago's vest?"

None of the men cared to venture a guess. Trying to raise Greg Hammond's spirits, Sergeant Chuck Foster said, "It's all right, Lieutenant. Sooner or later you'll kill Chago."

"Well, Sergeant, it had better be sooner," Hammond exclaimed as the troopers headed toward their horses, tethered near the rocks where they had been hiding. "Otherwise, innocent people will keep on dying at the hands of that vermin. All this killing—it's all such a waste, and I'll stop it or die trying!"

Sergeant Foster nodded sadly and, finding nothing to reply that would comfort the lieutenant, placed a reassuring hand on his elbow. Hammond acknowledged the gesture with a faint smile; then all of the men mounted up and rode in silence toward Fort McDowell.

Not far away a fourteen-year-old Apache youth, who had hidden his pinto at the bottom of a deep arroyo, watched from the crest of a rock as the white-eyes soldiers rode away. When they were out of sight, Eskamon swung onto his horse and headed for the village. He had heard Chago describe the soldier he hated so much—Lieutenant Greg Hammond—and Eskamon knew it was Hammond who had led the soldiers and blown Nachee and the other warriors to bits. And Tana, his mentor, was gone, too. Eskamon gritted his teeth in anger. Chago would *really* hate the white-eyes lieutenant now!

Three days passed, during which Hammond found himself heavily occupied. While carrying on his normal duties and trying to devise another plan to kill Chago, he kept a sharp eye on LuAnn Marlowe, to see if she was keeping her word and staying away from the colonel. He noticed that she seemed to have more time to visit with the other women in the fort, and one evening he saw her walking about the compound with Ella Yarrow, the sutler's wife. He was satisfied that their little talk had been what was needed. Apparently LuAnn had come to understand what she had been doing to the Ballard family as a whole, and she was changing her behavior accordingly.

Hammond spent as much time as possible with Anita, trying not to let her know that his mind at times wandered to Chago, wondering what form of retaliation the Apache leader might use to avenge the deaths of his brother and seven other Apaches.

At midmorning on the fourth day after the explosion of the coach, Hammond was ordered to report to the colonel. Corporal Graves ushered Hammond into the inner office and then returned to the outer office, closing the door.

Colonel Ballard was seated behind his desk, a cigarillo between his teeth and a solemn look on his face. Without giving a greeting, he lifted a telegram from his desk and handed it to Hammond. "Read this," he said coldly.

The lieutenant eyed the colonel noncommittally and then read the telegram. It had just come from the War Department in Washington, D.C., and Hammond at first thought it might contain some new directives for handling the Apaches. He was utterly unprepared for what the telegram in fact said: He was to be transferred immediately to Fort Abraham Lincoln in Dakota Territory, where he would be attached to one of the units engaged there in fighting the Sioux.

Hammond blanched as the message sank in. He understood its *real* import all too plainly. Whatever new officers were being dispatched to Fort McDowell had not yet arrived, and the fort was lacking in commissioned personnel. For the time being at least, Hammond was the senior officer under the commandant, and it made no sense to send him off to North Dakota when he was so obviously needed here.

A crimson flush crept over the lieutenant's face as he gazed at the colonel. His temper was building, but he kept his voice unruffled. "You engineered this, didn't you?"

Ballard regarded him with cold, calculating eyes, blowing smoke from the side of his mouth, but did not answer.

The silence between them thickened. Hammond growled, "Mrs. Marlowe told you of our conversation, didn't she?"

Ballard's reply seemed both resigned and bitter. "I'm sorry, Greg, I really am. I'm fond of you, as you know. But you stuck your nose in where it doesn't belong."

"She admitted the whole thing to me! Did she tell you that?"

"Yes, she told me."

"So then it's true, isn't it?" He paused, awaiting a reaction from Ballard; none came, and his silence could only mean assent. "Have you thought of what this is going to do to your wife, and also to Art and Anita?" Hammond went on. "What kind of a—"

"Keep your voice down!" snapped Ballard, sending an apprehensive glance toward the closed door. "I don't want Graves to hear this conversation."

"Why not?" rasped Hammond, his temper getting harder to control. "He's going to know all about this very soon anyway, unless this situation changes immediately. I suggest you get a telegram off to the War Department right now and have this order rescinded, or I'll expose you for what you are. Everyone on the post will hear about this, and I'll send a report to the brass in Washington, too. I wonder what they'll think of a commandant who cheats on his wife and carries on with the widow of an officer who died as a hero."

At first, rage seemed about to boil up in Ballard as his blazing eyes pierced Hammond. Then he calmed down and smiled sardonically. "You won't get anywhere with that gambit, Hammond. For one thing, I'll deny any report you make. And for another thing, I've heard Bill Radcliffe's report, and I can use it to finish your career."

Hammond bristled. "How so?"

"Your failure to let him kill Simino resulted in the deaths of eighteen men, including Captain Oatman. I'm not talking about the four men killed when you first pursued Chago and his savages; those losses are understandable. But from that experience you ought to have learned how tough Chago is, and you should have known he would come back with more warriors to rescue Simino. If I tell the brass in Washington that your poor and cowardly decision to spare Simino's life led to eighteen additional and unnecessary deaths, they'll court-martial you. And then any report you make about *my* activities will be thoroughly discredited—seen in fact as a craven attempt on your part to cover up your own derelictions as an officer. Your career will be finished!" Rising to his feet, Ballard added, "The best thing for you to do, Lieutenant, is to go quietly and take up your assignment at Fort Lincoln."

Hammond spoke through clenched teeth. "When I spared Simino's life, I was following army procedure to the letter, and you know it, Ballard! There are men in this fort who saw the incident, and they can testify to the facts. I'll stuff all that 'poor and cowardly' drivel down your adulterous throat!"

Ballard narrowed his eyes, pulled the burning cigarillo from his mouth, and pointed the red tip at Hammond. "Hammond, you know as well as I do that the army hates scandals, and even if you were acquitted at a court-martial— which I doubt—you'd never get a decent posting again. So I'm telling you once more: You have your orders from Washington, and you have no choice but to obey them at once. And one more thing: You're not to tell Anita anything except that you've been transferred. You got that?"

The lieutenant's pulse hammered at his temples. "I'll marry Anita immediately and take her with me!"

Ballard snarled, "You wouldn't dare!"

"Why not? She's of age, and she can make her own decisions. I didn't ask you if I could marry her because I had to. I did it out of respect for you—which, by the way, is all gone. I can't spare Anita the pain she's going to feel when she finds out about you, but at least I can remove her and spare her the shame of facing the men and women in this fort. You can count on it, Ballard. I'm going to Anita right now. We'll be husband and wife by tomorrow!"

"Try it and you're a dead man, Hammond!"

Greg squared his muscular shoulders. "You mean you'd actually try to kill me, Ballard?"

"I wouldn't have to. I've got men in this fort who would kill for me if I told them to. You make one move— any move at all—to try to take my daughter away from here, and you'll be planted in the cemetery with no gun salute and no taps. I'll make you look so bad that the army will write you off as a traitor. A black pall will hang over your grave, and Anita will hate your memory! I can do it, believe me!"

Hammond knew Ballard had the power to discredit him and ruin his army career. Whether he would actually arrange a murder was questionable; he was probably bluffing on that part. But Greg had no way to be sure. Colonel Ballard was not the criminal type, but he might do something desperate if cornered, and there might be some hard-bitten recruit on base who would be willing to risk a quick and dirty way to fast advancement. . . .

Whatever the case, Hammond was going to be torn from the woman he loved and sent to Fort Lincoln, and he could do nothing about it.

Ballard's threats had taken root, and the colonel could see it on Hammond's face. Jamming the cigarillo back between his teeth, he said, this time a shade less angrily, "You and Anita will forget each other in time. Just go quietly and don't make any waves . . . that's my final word on the subject."

Regarding the colonel coldly, Hammond said, "So how soon do you expect me to leave?"

"Right now. The orders said immediately."

"You think the men in this fort are going to believe that the army would order me to leave before replacement officers have arrived? You and I know things don't usually happen that way, and so do the men."

"I can convince them that it's an emergency," commented Ballard. "Everybody here has kept up with what's going on with Sitting Bull and Crazy Horse and all those hotheaded Sioux. There's a big confrontation coming, as sure as anything, and it's likely to make our Apache troubles seem like a Sunday-school picnic. So the army needs a rough and tough lieutenant like you—needs him real bad. Everyone knows that seasoned officers are always in short supply in peacetime, so the army has to stretch itself thin. The men will believe that, and I can make Anita believe it, too. In fact, while you're packing, I'll go break the news to her. Then you two can have your little good-bye session, and you'll be on your way."

Hammond rose to his feet, his feelings of rage boiling to the surface. "Ballard, I can see you have this all figured out. You have me where you want me, and I'll go. But if there's ever any way I can get even with you, you can be sure I will!"

The colonel regarded him coolly, saying nothing.

"By the way," Hammond went on, "no stagecoaches are moving through Apache Junction right now. I'll need to catch a northbound stage out of Phoenix, so I guess I'll have to ride all the way there on an army horse. What do you expect me to do with it?"

"I'll have a couple of men escort you. They can bring it back. Now, you get packed. I'll go tell Anita."

Still fuming, Hammond had just finished packing his bag when there was a knock at his door. When he pulled the door open, Anita, her face tear-stained, crossed the threshold and plunged into his arms.

Clinging tightly to him, the lovely redhead sobbed, "Oh, Greg! I can't bear this! How could those awful men in Washington do this to us?"

Hammond ached to tell her the truth, but he swallowed the words he wanted to say and spoke with a level voice. "The army doesn't have feelings, darling. They just have Indians to fight. All that matters to the bigwigs behind their desks in Washington is that men are needed to fight the Sioux right now."

"But Dad says he doesn't even know if you can be reassigned here when the Sioux troubles are over. Greg, my darling, you must come back! If you don't, I'll come to wherever you are!"

Hammond had already made up his mind that in spite of Colonel Philip Ballard he would return as soon as possible and take Anita away with him. They would marry and have their life together. But for the present, there was nothing he could do. Holding her close, he said, "I will write as often as I can, darling, and once the Sioux are under control, we'll make plans for our wedding. I'll miss you something fierce, but we'll be back together soon."

"Oh, Greg, I'll miss you, too!" exclaimed Anita, unable to stop weeping. "I love you so very much!"

She was just bringing her emotions under control when her father appeared at the door and said, "The men are ready, Lieutenant."

Hammond glared at Ballard over Anita's shoulder, and then he kissed her and followed the commandant outside.

Word had spread quickly through the fort that Lieutenant Hammond had received orders to report to Fort Abraham Lincoln as soon as possible, and the men in blue had gathered informally on the parade ground, where two troopers waited to escort Hammond to Phoenix.

Though Hammond's betrothal to Anita had not been announced, their love was no secret, and word of the impending engagement had inevitably leaked out, too. Esther Ballard did not hesitate to embrace and kiss the lieutenant openly, as if he were already a member of the family, and Art stepped forward to shake his hand warmly.

The colonel had obviously not yet told his family that he expected Anita to forget Hammond in time and break off the engagement.

Then the lieutenant spoke with the men as they crowded around and expressed their regret that he was being transferred. With many a backslap they wished him luck and a speedy return.

Philip Ballard put on a hypocritical smile, laid a hand on the lieutenant's shoulder, and told him in front of the crowd that he would miss him. Esther embraced Greg again, telling him that she would look forward to the day when he would return to marry Anita, and Art urged him to be careful, for he was looking forward to having a brother-in-law.

Anita had been standing back, her eyes brimming with tears, but finally Hammond took her in his arms and kissed her soundly. There was a stirring of approval among the men, as well as a few cheers. "I love you, Anita," Hammond whispered to her. "I will be back to make you my bride."

"And I will be waiting," she said shakily through her tears.

They kissed again, and Hammond swung into the saddle. His luggage was anchored to the cantle. The lieutenant kneed his mount forward, his two escorts following. When they reached the gate Hammond turned around in the saddle and raised a hand in farewell to the woman he loved. He could see her weeping intensify as she waved back, handkerchief in hand. Steeling himself, Hammond turned again and, with a glance at his companions, rode through the gate and out of sight.

Standing disconsolately on the parade ground as she watched her man ride from view, Anita felt her father's arm around her. She knew he was trying to console her, but something made her tremble at the touch. Still unable to believe that her happiness had been dashed to bits in so short a time, she glanced about dazedly. The men had begun to disperse, talking among themselves in low tones. She saw LuAnn Marlowe standing on the porch of the sutler's store, her expression unreadable except for a faint smile. Then she caught sight of Lieutenant Bill Radcliffe peering through the window of the infirmary, seemingly smiling as well. Consumed by her own sorrow, not knowing or caring about anything else, she broke free of her father's arm and ran all the way to the Ballards' house.

The still-tearful young woman dashed into the house and up to her room. She pulled a small calendar off the wall and carried it to her bed. Sitting down, she wiped away her tears and pressed a finger on the day's date . . . May 3, 1876. "Oh, Greg, how long will it be until I am in your arms again?"

On the twenty-ninth of May, Esther Ballard was beginning to prepare the evening meal. She heard the front door open and looked up as Anita entered the kitchen, a few envelopes in her hand. "I have the mail, Mother. And look what I got!"

Placing the other letters on a counter, she held up one that was addressed to her, with the name Lieutenant Gregory L. Hammond in the upper corner.

"A letter from Greg!" cried Esther, clapping her hands with delight. "Well, open it, dear!"

"I will," smiled Anita. "But if you don't mind, I'll do it in my room." She took the letter and disappeared.

When the colonel came home a few moments later, Esther told him about the letter. He said nothing but looked away, a frown etching his forehead. Shortly afterward Art also came in, and when he learned about the letter he let out a whoop of joy.

Moments later Anita emerged from her room, drying her eyes. She had been crying, and Esther went to her and put her arm around her shoulders. "What's wrong, dear? Is Greg all right?"

"He's fine, Mother," sniffed Anita.

"Well, what are you crying about?" asked the colonel.

"Oh, Dad," she replied as fresh tears brimmed in her eyes, "I just miss him so much. No one will ever know how very much I love him, more and more as each day passes."

"Did he say anything of interest in the letter?" Ballard asked offhandedly.

"Well, the most interesting words are personal for *me*, Dad," she said. "But he did say that he's been attached to the Seventh Cavalry to serve under Lieutenant Colonel George Armstrong Custer."

"Custer, eh?" said Ballard, smiling. "Well, he's a colorful character. Controversial, but highly regarded in some quarters. It's a feather in Greg's cap to be riding with him—definitely a step up. He'll probably see lots of action, too."

Esther sent her husband a sharp glance as she set out the supper. "Now, Philip Ballard, that's enough of such talk! We don't want to worry the poor child any more than we have to." She turned to Anita. "I'm sure Greg will be just fine, dear. Now, all of you, let's sit down and eat. I think we could do with a good hot meal. Art, will you say the blessing?"

The next morning Colonel Ballard entered the mail office where Sergeant Francis O'Malley was doing some paperwork. "Good morning, sir. What can I do for you?" the sergeant cheerfully asked.

"Just a simple thing," said Ballard. "From now on, I don't want any more of Lieutenant Hammond's letters to reach my daughter. When you find them in the mail, pass them along to me. Is that clear?"

"Well, yes, sir," replied the sergeant with a puzzled look on his face. "But I don't understand, Colonel. She knows when the mail comes in, and she's usually here waiting for it—"

"You have to sort it first, don't you, before you can distribute it?"

"Well, yes, but—"

"Good. Then it should be a simple matter simply to set aside any letter from the lieutenant without her seeing what you're doing. That's an order."

The sergeant shook his head doubtfully.

Ballard leaned forward over the counter and spoke in a confidental tone. "Sergeant, you have your orders, and that's all you need. But I can understand your curiosity, so I'll tell you confidentially that I've found out on good authority that Hammond has already got himself a lady friend at Fort Lincoln. He's stringing Anita along, just to feed his rotten ego, while he carries on with this other woman."

O'Malley's eyes opened wide. "Why, sir, that seems impossible! The lieutenant never seemed to be that kind of guy, and—"

"Believe me, it's true, Sergeant, and no one could be sorrier about it than I am. So, no more of his letters get through to my daughter, right? You bring them to me. I don't want her getting hurt. I'll decide when the time is right to break the bad news to her."

"I understand, sir. I'm real sorry. What a thing to have happen. . . . I still can't believe it!"

As May gave way to June, LuAnn Marlowe continued to meet Philip Ballard secretly, biding her time, still determined to do away with Esther Ballard.

During one of their amorous encounters, Ballard told LuAnn about his instructions to the sergeant. He also confided that Lieutenant Bill Radcliffe, now fully recovered from his wound, had become interested in his daughter, a development he was encouraging. Anita, still upset and lonely, needed the distraction, the colonel said, and he was hoping something more would come of it. Anita, for her part, was treating Radcliffe kindly, making it plain that she was not interested in anything beyond a friendly relationship. She still insisted that she was in love with Greg Hammond and considered herself engaged to him, but at least she was accepting Radcliffe's social calls.

LuAnn smiled to herself when she heard all of this. Like LuAnn, Bill Radcliffe was something of an opportunist and obviously knew how to turn a situation to his own advantage. They were two of a kind, she decided.

"Will you tell Anita that story you told the sergeant?" she asked Hammond pointedly. "I mean about Hammond's supposed other woman?"

"I don't know," Ballard replied. "I'm hoping I won't have to. If Bill Radcliffe's half the man I think he is, he'll solve the problem for me. I'm thinking Anita will just forget about Greg Hammond in time—maybe even before the summer's out."

"And if she doesn't?" LuAnn insisted. "Will you tell her?"

Hammond looked at her bitterly. "LuAnn, I got rid of Hammond, as you suggested—insisted, in fact. I knew I had to do it if we were going to go on seeing each other, but I hope it stops there. I don't want to hurt my own daughter any more than I already have."

Chapter Thirteen

Late in the morning of June 25, Chago returned to his village from his journey to the northern Arizona mountains. He had settled the conflict among the Jicarillas, selecting a successor to Chief Ramino who would be satisfactory to all. He had conveyed Amanzus's good wishes to Ramino, and he had also been present during the dying chief's final hours and the subsequent burial ceremonies.

Before he died, Ramino thanked Chago for his efforts on behalf of the Jicarillas, and he also cautioned the young warrior that the old ways of the Apache could not remain unchanged forever. Inevitably, he warned, a day would come when the Apaches would have to lay down their weapons and learn to live in peace with the white man. At these words Chago bristled, though he said nothing in the presence of the dying man, whom he had always respected. But once outside Ramino's hut, he spat on the ground in contempt for such weakness.

Upon his return home Chago's somber mood turned into deeper sorrow and bitter wrath when he was informed of his brother's death. Young Eskamon made sure Chago knew that it was Lieutenant Greg Hammond who had led

the soldiers the day Nachee and the others were blown up
at the abandoned stagecoach.

Cursing Hammond by his gods, Chago retreated to
his private hut, brooding over schemes to get revenge.
Before a dirty mirror that hung on a post in his shack,
Chago studied his own face, so similar to Nachee's except
for the ugly scar that Hammond had put there. More than
ever he was obsessed with the desire to kill the lieutenant,
and until he had personally taken Hammond's life, Chago
would not rest.

When he emerged from his hut, Chago—over Amanzus's
objections—immediately assembled a band of bloodthirsty
warriors to help him take vengeance on the white-eyes
soldiers. Chago could wait no longer; the desire for revenge
burned so deep within him that he demanded the warriors
break with Apache custom and launch a surprise attack
after dark. A few grumbled at this, in fear for their souls
should they perish after sundown, but Chago's strong will
and charisma prevailed. The white-eyes would not be
expecting the attack, he pointed out, and the element of
surprise would be so greatly in the Apaches' favor that no
warriors would be killed. The young braves, many of
whom were inclined like Chago to question the ancient
tribal beliefs, accepted his persuasive arguments.

The plan was simple: They would go over the stockade
wall, guns blazing, and if Chago did not see Hammond
right away, he would force a soldier to take him to him.
While the other warriors were keeping the soldiers busy—
but not risking their own lives unduly—Chago would find
and execute the hated lieutenant. Once it was done, he
would give a shrill whistle that could be heard above
gunfire, and they would all retreat to the walls, climb over
them, and ride away into the night.

Chago asked Simino to go along, but Simino declined,
saying he was not yet ready for hand-to-hand battle. His
shoulder was still giving him some trouble.

*   *   *

When Colonel Ballard had wired the War Department in Washington to request Hammond's transfer, he had also put in for two new captains and one new lieutenant, superseding his earlier request when he had been planning to promote Hammond to captain. The two new captains, Mitchell Payne and Donald Cruz, arrived early in June along with their families, as did the new lieutenant and some twenty new troopers.

It was just past ten o'clock on the night of the twenty-fifth when LuAnn Marlowe walked casually across the parade ground, having just spent a few moments with Philip Ballard in his office. As she neared her quarters she paused to exchange greetings with several people who were out taking the cool night air, among them the captains and their wives and children. The officers greeted her cordially, saying kind words about Dan Marlowe and what a hero he had been.

LuAnn entered her rooms, lighted a lantern, and was heading for the bedroom when a sudden blast of gunfire and the whoops of Apaches sounded outside. Then she heard the bugler at the tower blowing the signal for all women and children to run to the number one supply building, the site designated as a shelter for noncombatants in the event of attack. Like all the other buildings in the compound, a blazing lantern clearly marked its entrance.

Quickly LuAnn ran to an oak bureau, opened a drawer, and found her dead husband's service revolver. Withdrawing the gun from its holster, she broke it open to check that it was fully loaded and then snapped it shut. Still carrying the revolver, she dashed out of the house and headed across the compound for the supply building. All around her she could see the flashes of gunpowder and hear the guns roar as whites and Indians did battle. Running as fast as she could, she found herself pulling up behind Esther Ballard and her daughter, also headed for the supply building. Ahead of them were the captains' wives and children, being guided by Ella Yarrow. Every one of the women was carrying a revolver.

Bullets were flying all around, some biting the ground near their feet and some hitting the supply building. Ella Yarrow passed through the door, urging those behind her to hurry. The captains' wives propelled their children through the doorway and then plunged in after them just as Esther and Anita Ballard were within twenty feet of the building.

Suddenly LuAnn Marlowe saw her chance. Esther was now pushing Anita in front of her, anxious to get her daughter out of danger ahead of herself. Her back presented a perfect target.

LuAnn cocked the gun and raised it just as a stray bullet whizzed by her head. Telling herself that with the bullets hissing all around, the colonel would readily believe that an Apache had shot Esther, she took quick aim and fired the gun. The slug entered Esther's back, and she fell just outside the door. At the sound of her fall Anita turned around in the doorway and screamed.

Covering for herself, LuAnn whipped around and fired into the deep shadows. "I saw the Apache who shot her, Anita!" she shouted, firing once more and then quickly coming over to where Esther lay.

Anita was stunned. Laying aside the gun she was carrying, she placed her arms under her mother's shoulders and looked pleadingly at LuAnn. "Help me get her inside!"

Keeping the gun in her hand, LuAnn complied, and once they had Esther inside the door, LuAnn closed it. To her great regret she saw that Philip Ballard's wife was still breathing.

Outside, guns boomed, soldiers shouted, and Apaches whooped. Chago saw the colonel, aided by two captains he did not recognize, directing the defense against the sudden attack. The colonel was skillfully deploying his men, using them to good advantage, but as Chago had promised, the element of surprise was working in the Apaches' favor. The warriors, as Chago had instructed, were fighting defensively, firing from cover rather than charging their enemy in the open, since their main intent was simply to distract the soldiers and pin them down while Chago sought out Hammond.

Chago ducked between two buildings, searching for the despised lieutenant. Suddenly he came face to face with a young trooper. Battle wise and fast on his feet, Chago slammed the young man with the butt of his rifle, knocking him down, and then kicked the soldier's rifle out of reach and jumped on top of him, pressing a knife to his throat.

The dazed soldier's expression was one of pure terror as the determined Apache ordered, "Tell me where I can find Lieutenant Greg Hammond!"

The trooper swallowed hard. "He ain't here!"

Believing the man to be lying, Chago nicked the skin of the soldier's throat and demanded, "I ask you once more. Where is Hammond?"

"I'm tellin' the truth!" the soldier gasped frantically. "Lieutenant Hammond was sent to Dakota Territory to fight the Sioux!"

Enraged by this unexpected development, Chago swore and, holding the trooper's head by the hair, buried the knife in his throat. He withdrew the knife and dropped the dead man's head in the dirt; then he rose and headed for the nearest wall, giving a shrill whistle as he ran.

Colonel Ballard looked around him, startled at the sudden cessation of hostilities. Within less than a minute all the Apaches had fled except for two who had fallen under army fire.

Gathering all of the men on the parade ground, Ballard and his officers made a count of the casualties, while Dr. Wheatley arrived and began to attend to the wounded.

Two soldiers had hurried to the supply building to check on the women and children, and one of them came running back, out of breath as he gasped, "Colonel Ballard! Your wife's been hit!"

His face white, Ballard followed the soldier to the building, where he found Esther unconscious and Anita and LuAnn hovering over her. LuAnn told him quickly that an Apache bullet had caught Esther in the back just as they were all trying to get inside the building.

At the colonel's orders a stretcher was brought, and two soldiers gently carried Esther to the infirmary, with the colonel, Anita, and LuAnn following behind.

Art showed up soon afterward. Having been caught outside during the attack, he had seized a fallen trooper's revolver and gotten off some shots at the Apaches, though he had failed to hit any. He had come running as soon as he heard the news about his mother.

Doc Wheatley, who by now had quickly patched up the wounded men and was having them transported to the infirmary, examined Esther's wound. Shaking his head, he summoned the orderly who regularly assisted him at surgery.

"I'll do the best I can for her," he told Ballard compassionately, "but I can't give you a lot of hope. The bullet must have been fired from very close range, because it's in deep. Now, I'll have to ask you to wait in the outer room while I do my work. I'll let you know just as soon as I'm done."

LuAnn Marlowe waited with the family while the surgery was being performed. She and the colonel said very little to each other, though she spoke soothing words to Anita and Art.

Only ten minutes had passed when the door opened. They all rose to their feet, knowing that the surgery could not have been finished yet. Anita's hand went to her mouth and her face was drawn.

The doctor came through the door, his face devoid of color. Running his dull gaze over their faces, he said, "I . . . I'm sorry, I couldn't save her. The bullet went deep enough in her back to damage the heart, and she died while I was probing for the slug."

Weeping, Anita and Art clung to their father. LuAnn expressed her sorrow in polite terms; then, with a meaningful glance at the colonel, she excused herself and left.

The colonel and his two children reentered the infirmary to be with Esther for a moment of farewell. While they were standing there, Wheatley drew the colonel to one side. "I want to show you something," he said.

Curious, Anita and Art approached and looked on, all three of them watching as the doctor went to a counter near the operating table and picked up the bullet that he had removed from Esther's back. Laying it in the palm of Ballard's hand, he asked, "What can you tell me about this slug, Colonel?"

"It's forty-five caliber," replied Ballard instantly.

"From what kind of weapon?"

"A revolver—yes, it would have to be a revolver."

"Dad," Art spoke up, "Apaches don't use revolvers in battle. They always use rifles if they're going to use a gun."

"You're right, son," nodded Ballard.

Anita was puzzled. "What does this mean, Dad?"

"I'm not sure, dear," said the colonel. "It doesn't make sense."

The colonel's mind was whirring. He knew the women were all supposed to carry guns during an attack, and LuAnn had still been carrying hers when she had left a few moments earlier.

"Well," said the doctor, "I guess it can only mean one thing. Some Apache broke the rule. He was using a forty-five-caliber revolver."

*   *   *

With the exception of the wounded men, virtually the entire fort turned out for the burial the next morning. Colonel Philip Ballard looked at the neat, rectangular holes in the earth, for his fallen men and for his wife, and wondered if Chago would be satisfied. He doubted it. No doubt more blood would be shed over the Nachee incident.

When the ceremony was finished and taps had been played, the men came forward one by one to offer their sympathies to the colonel and his family. LuAnn, too, approached, briefly embraced Anita and Art, and then shook Ballard's hand. She gave it an extra squeeze and gazed into his eyes, her expression appropriately somber except for a slight upturn at the corners of her lips.

After the soldiers and LuAnn had moved away, Anita stood alone for a brief moment, weeping softly. Lieutenant Bill Radcliffe drew close to her and said, "I'm awfully sorry, Anita. You know I'm here, and if there's anything I can do . . ."

Anita raised her eyes to his and then broke down completely, sobbing uncontrollably. She took a step forward, stumbled, and Radcliffe reached out to support her. He held her, and she leaned her head on his shoulder, still crying.

"If . . . only . . . Greg were here," she murmured, her voice so soft and choked that Radcliffe was not certain she had even spoken.

That evening, while Art and Anita sat disconsolately in the parlor, the colonel, saying he had some things to attend to at the office, left the house. He directed his steps toward LuAnn's quarters.

When she answered his knock, LuAnn smiled broadly and welcomed him in. Closing the door after he had entered, she said, "I knew you would come tonight!" She pressed herself against him and planted a soft, warm kiss on his lips. When she realized he was not responding, she withdrew to arm's length and looked at him. Ballard's face was like granite. "What's the matter, darling?" she asked.

"LuAnn," he said, his voice bitter, "I buried the mother of my children today."

"I know that, dear," she replied, taking his hands in hers. "It was a terrible shock. But it's going to be all right now." She embraced him. "You love me, and I'm alive, here for you always. When the time's right—you know, after a decent interval—we can be married. I can be the wife of Colonel Philip Ballard, commandant of Fort McDowell—"

"LuAnn," Ballard demanded abruptly, pushing her back so he could look into her eyes, "did you see the Apache that shot Esther?"

"Certainly. Didn't Anita tell you? I shot at him as he was vanishing into the darkness."

Ballard regarded the beautiful woman with grim suspicion. "Anita didn't say anything about that. What kind of a gun did the Apache have?"

LuAnn cocked her head sideways and furrowed her brow. "I don't know, Phil. It happened so fast, and I'm not too well educated about guns."

"You know a rifle from a handgun, don't you?"

"Well, of course."

"Which was it?"

"Why, it must have been a rifle. Isn't that what all Indians use? I remember hearing Dan talk about that."

"Did you say you shot at the Apache?" pressed Ballard.

"Yes," she nodded, heading for the bureau where the revolver was kept. "I shot at him twice, but I haven't fired a gun more than three or four times in my life. I'm not a very good shot. I must have missed him, because I never saw him again."

While she was speaking, LuAnn pulled out the revolver and handed it to the colonel. Noting its caliber, Ballard broke it open and examined the cartridge heads carefully. Two of them had firing-pin marks, indicating they had been discharged, leaving behind only the empty shells. Snapping the gun shut, he handed it back to her and looked into her face with troubled eyes.

LuAnn laid the weapon on top of the bureau and then wrapped her arms around him and said softly, "Darling, I can understand that you're upset. It couldn't have been easy for you to have Esther die that way."

A frown crossed his forehead. Pushing LuAnn to arm's length again, he said flatly, "LuAnn, the bullet that killed Esther was from a forty-five caliber revolver."

"I didn't know there was a difference between a bullet from a rifle and one from a revolver," LuAnn said in an innocent tone. "If they're both the same caliber, how can you tell the difference?"

"It's quite simple. The diameter of the bullet is the same, but a rifle cartridge is longer so it can hold more gunpowder. The slug that it carries is longer too, and heavier. Now, I saw the slug that came out of Esther's body, and it came from a revolver. Since Apaches don't use pistols in battle, as Dan told you, wouldn't you say it was someone other than an Apache who shot Esther?"

LuAnn hesitated and then stammered, "Well, I . . . I d-don't know. . . . Oh, Phil! There were bullets flying all around us. You don't suppose one of the officer's shots went wild? I—I m-mean . . . that Esther's death was . . . an accident?"

"You tell me." Ballard's tone was icy.

The woman's lips quivered. "Wh-what do you mean?"

"Anita told me you were directly behind them. Did she tell it correctly?"

"Why, yes. Yes, I was right behind them."

"Doc Wheatley told me that the shot came from close range. Since the Apache you saw had a rifle, he couldn't have been the one who shot Esther. If one of the officers had put a bullet in her—accidentally, of course—he would have had to be plenty close to you. Did you see him?"

"Well, no . . . I—"

"Not only that, but in order for the officer to have hit Esther without hitting you, his bullet would have had to enter Esther's body from an angle. But it went in straight, meaning that whoever fired the gun was not only very close, but *directly* behind her."

LuAnn Marlowe's expression now was that of a cornered animal. She was silent for a moment, sweat beading her brow, and then she embraced him wildly. "All right! All right! So I killed her! It was only because I so desperately want to be your wife, darling! Surely you can't fault me for that. I love you, Philip! I love y—"

Ballard pushed LuAnn away so roughly that she stumbled backward. "We're through, LuAnn!" he blurted, heading for the door.

"Philip!" she screamed, shaking her fists. "You don't mean that!"

Stopping about ten feet from the door, Ballard pivoted. Trembling with rage, he pointed a stiff finger at her. "Pack up and get out of the fort, or I'll have you hanged for murder!"

As Ballard wheeled about to move toward the door, LuAnn grabbed the revolver from the top of the bureau and snapped back the hammer. Ballard halted in his tracks and spun around. Behind the ominous black muzzle he saw wild, murderous eyes.

"LuAnn! Put that gun down!"

The furious, trembling woman glared at him along the barrel, which she was struggling to hold steady. "I hate you!" she hissed. At the same time, she squeezed the trigger.

The impact of the .45-caliber slug knocked Ballard

down, though it had hit him on the tip of his left shoulder. Clawing for the service revolver on his hip, he drew it and dogged back the hammer. Before he could fire the gun, LuAnn took two steps closer and shot him again.

The second bullet slammed into his chest, knocking the breath out of him. The raging blonde cocked her revolver again, but in spite of his wounds Ballard was able to level his own weapon at her heart and fire.

The room was foggy with gunsmoke as LuAnn Marlowe was blasted back against the bureau. She hovered there for a few seconds before slumping to the floor.

Heavy boots pounded on the steps outside and the door burst open. Three troopers charged in, pistols drawn, fearing that an Apache might have hidden in the apartment and shot Mrs. Marlowe. They were shocked to see their commandant lying on the floor near the door with two bleeding wounds, and the widow lying dead across the room.

Ballard was conscious, and two of the troopers did what they could to make him comfortable while the other one ran for Doc Wheatley. By the time Wheatley arrived, carrying his black bag, more men had gathered outside the apartment door, including the captains, who ordered all except the two troopers who had found Ballard to stay out of the room.

Doc Wheatley strode through the door, took one look at the dead woman, and then went over to kneel beside Ballard. Speaking in a low tone, he said to the troopers, "Better bring Anita and Art . . . and make it fast. He doesn't have long."

Ballard coughed and looked up at the doctor with glazed eyes. "Did I hear you right, Doc?"

"You did," Wheatley replied solemnly.

The colonel's features contorted with pain and the shock of Wheatley's unequivocal answer.

Anita and Art Ballard arrived within two minutes. As they knelt down, tears ran down their cheeks as Ballard licked his lips and coughed. "Anita . . . Art . . . I must tell you . . . I did you and your mother wrong. I . . . LuAnn and I were seeing each other. . . . A year now. She killed your mother . . . so the two of us could . . . could marry. I just made her admit it, and she went wild."

"Oh, Daddy," Anita cried. "Why? Why—?"

"Listen to me, honey," Ballard said hoarsely. "I did an awful thing to you. Greg . . . Greg found out about our affair. He threatened to expose us if we didn't break it off. LuAnn insisted I get him transferred, so . . . so I did."

"Oh-h-h-!" sobbed Anita, shaking her head as if she were in a wild nightmare.

Ballard coughed again and blood appeared at the corners of his mouth. Choking on it, he gasped, "Honey, please . . . please forgive me! Please, Anita! You must say you will for—"

Suddenly the colonel coughed once more, and then he went limp.

Doc Wheatley laid one hand on Anita's shoulder and the other on Art's. "He's gone," he said softly.

Brother and sister wrapped their arms around each other, held on, and cried incoherently.

The next morning, June 27, 1876, a grieving Anita Ballard wrote a letter to Greg Hammond telling what had happened, including her dying father's confession of the affair with LuAnn Marlowe and of his sending Greg away. With tears in her eyes and her hand trembling as she wrote, Anita begged Greg to request transfer back to Fort McDowell, for she needed him desperately.

Anita posted the letter at the mail office as she and Art walked toward the cemetery for the burial of their father. By then everyone in the fort knew about the colonel's affair with LuAnn Marlowe, and their hearts went out to Art and Anita.

As brother and sister passed through the gate to the cemetery, Lieutenant Bill Radcliffe drew alongside them and offered his sympathies. When Anita began to weep, Radcliffe put an arm around her shoulders. Her heart heavy beyond bearing at this second funeral in as many days, Anita accepted his kindness, but Art stayed apart, glaring at Radcliffe coldly.

The lieutenant stayed close to Anita during the funeral service, which was conducted by Captain Mitchell Payne, who as the senior captain was now acting commandant until a new one could be assigned to the fort.

Having known the colonel only a brief time, Captain Payne kept his eulogy short, preferring to adhere to the Scriptures that might comfort the twice-afflicted family. He read the Thirty-Ninth Psalm, and Anita wept audibly as she heard the words, " 'And now, Lord, what wait I for? My hope is in thee. Deliver me from all my transgressions. . . .' "

After the service the captain stepped over to Anita, expressed his condolences, and offered to escort her home. Radcliffe politely intervened and said that he would be glad to perform this service, and the captain graciously yielded.

Radcliffe and Anita, followed by Art, whom the lieutenant barely acknowledged, made their way to the Ballard home. Anita thanked Radcliffe for his thoughtfulness and then entered the house with her brother.

LuAnn Marlowe was also buried that day. Captain Payne asked Captain Cruz to be at the graveside; otherwise, only the burial crew was in attendance.

A week later, on July 4, while the men at the post were preparing to observe Independence Day, Sergeant Chuck Foster was in Captain Payne's office as the dispatcher from the telegraph office came in with a wire. "Bad news, sir," the dispatcher said as he handed the paper to Payne.

Sergeant Foster watched the captain's face turn white as he read the telegram. "What is it, sir?" he asked.

"The Seventh Cavalry," Payne said weakly. "It was totally annihilated on the twenty-fifth of last month by Chief Crazy Horse and several thousand Sioux at the Little Bighorn River in southern Montana."

"The *Seventh!*" gasped Foster. "That . . . that was Colonel Custer!"

"Custer was killed, too," mumbled Payne sadly. "Not one man of the Seventh lived."

Foster rubbed a shaky hand across his mouth. "Sir," he said, "is there any possibility of error here? I mean, that some of the men in the Seventh could have survived?"

"I'm afraid not, Sergeant," replied the captain. "The army doesn't notify all its posts of a thing like this unless they have the facts confirmed. The twenty-fifth . . . that's the same day Chago and his men stormed the fort. Curious coincidence." Shaking his head, the captain rose and went to look out his window. "Those poor men. I feel for their families. It must have taken days for word to get back from the Little Bighorn, and that's obviously why it's taken this long for the news to get onto the wires."

Foster made a quick explanation to Payne about Anita Ballard's engagement to Lieutenant Greg Hammond, who had been transferred to Fort Abraham Lincoln and attached to Custer's Seventh Cavalry. Payne commented that someone should tell Anita right away, for she had a right to know.

"I'll be glad to speak with her," Foster said. "I've known the family for a long time."

"Thank you, Sergeant, I appreciate that," the captain acknowledged. "Of course I must go myself, because that's my duty as acting commandant. But I'd be grateful to have you along, since hearing it from you might make it easier for Miss Ballard."

The two men headed toward the Ballard home, where they found Lieutenant Radcliffe seated with Anita on the front porch. When the beautiful redhead observed the new visitors' faces, she knew something was wrong.

The captain spoke first. "Ma'am, I'm sorry to intrude, but we've just received word . . ."

Foster stepped forward as if on cue. "Anita, darlin'," he said with quivering lips, "somethin' bad has happened. We . . . hate to bring more bad news, after all your heartache, but you've got to know."

Fear came over Anita's pale face. She glanced at the telegram in the captain's hand and then said, "It's not . . . it's not Greg, is it? I haven't heard from him in weeks, and I've been wondering . . ."

The sergeant's eyes were brimming with tears. "Honey, I'm afraid— He—"

Foster could say nothing more. Frustrated, he took the telegram from the captain and handed it to Anita. Rising to accept it, she read it slowly.

As the message began to sink in, Anita's eyes took on a faraway look. She dropped the telegram, faltered a step, and then collapsed in a dead faint.

When she came to a moment later, Bill Radcliffe was holding her in his arms; the captain and sergeant were still present, and Art Ballard had come onto the porch. When the awful truth hit her mind again she wept inconsolably, and Radcliffe gently helped her up and guided her into the house. There he held her close, telling her over and over again that he was in love with her. He would take care of her.

Five days later Colonel William Branson, the new permanent commandant, arrived at Fort McDowell. He confirmed the order—already issued by Mitchell—that patrols should continue to look for Chago. The bloody Apache must be brought to ground.

He also paid an immediate call on Anita and Art Ballard, expressing his profoundest regrets over the losses in their family and offering to help them in any way he could. He assured them that he was in no hurry to occupy the commandant's house; as a bachelor he was content to stay for the time being in the single officers' compound.

In the days that followed, Anita found that Lieutenant Radcliffe seemed to have plenty of spare time to devote to her, and in spite of Art, who made no secret of his dislike for the lieutenant, she found herself responding to Radcliffe's kindness, warming up to him more and more every day.

Three weeks from the day Anita had learned of the Seventh Cavalry's annihilation, Radcliffe proposed marriage. Anita, still in the depths of despondency over all the tragic incidents that had occurred, weighed the matter. Greg Hammond was gone forever, her parents were dead, and Radcliffe had been there when she needed strength and help. In her dejected state of mind, having no prospects and nowhere to go, she could not refuse the proposal.

Art at first seemed depressed over her decision, but she persuaded him that Bill had been a real help to her and she needed him, and he accepted his sister's decision.

Bill and Anita were married on August 5. In the absence of her father, and in his memory—for in her heart she had forgiven him—Anita chose to walk down the aisle alone. Art stood beside the groom, acting as best man.

Around midmorning on a day two weeks later, lovely Anita Radcliffe was walking across the parade ground when her attention was drawn to an army wagon pulling through the gate. The sunlight was dancing on her auburn hair as she suddenly stopped in her tracks, her eyes focusing on the face of a blue-uniformed man riding next to the driver. She swallowed hard, unable to believe her eyes. Her heart seemed to stop. Alighting from the wagon and smiling at her was *Greg Hammond!*

Hammond ran to her, shouting, "Anita, darling!"

As soldiers stood around watching in shocked surprise, Anita felt her head begin to swim. Greg folded her in his arms; not knowing how to respond, Anita felt her body go limp.

"Anita!" he gasped. "What's wrong?"

"Greg," she said with difficulty, "I . . . thought you were dead."

"Dead . . . what do you mean?"

"Yes. I . . . I was told that every man in the Seventh Cavalry was killed at the Little Bighorn."

Looking at her askance, he said, "Didn't you get my letters?"

"I got the one you wrote when you first arrived at Fort Lincoln, saying that you had been attached to the Seventh Cavalry under Colonel Custer."

"And that's all?"

"Yes. Are you saying you wrote more letters?"

"Yes, of course! I wrote you just a few days after the first letter to tell you that I had been reassigned to another unit. I've written eight, maybe ten letters since."

Anita was feeling sick inside. "Oh, Greg—"

"Darling, no wonder you look so shocked. But it's all right now. I'm alive, and we're together! When I received your letter telling of your parents' deaths, I immediately requested assignment back here to Fort McDowell. It took a long time for the transfer to go through—the top brass has been real busy since the loss of Custer and his men—but it's all worked out now! We can get married! And I guess you can see by the bars on my shoulder that they've made me a captain!"

Greg Hammond jubilantly pulled her close, and Anita's heart went cold. Her tongue was frozen, and she was at a total loss as to how to break the terrible news to him.

Suddenly a cold voice cut the air. "Hammond! What in the name of heaven—" Bill Radcliffe was striding across the parade ground. "We thought you had been killed. How did you get back here? And while we're at it, that's my wife you're embracing! I'll thank you to stand off!"

At the sound of Radcliffe's voice Hammond jerked his head around. Glaring at the lieutenant, he released Anita, who backed away and stood motionless. His face was chalky and his eyes filled with disbelief as he looked at her and then at Radcliffe.

The lieutenant stepped to his wife's side and put an arm around her shoulder. Regarding Hammond with leaden eyes, he said, "If you had cared anything about her, you'd have written so she would know you were still alive. Well, it's too late; she's now Mrs. William Radcliffe!"

Leaving the couple standing on the parade ground, Hammond turned on his heel, walked stiff-leggedly to the mail office, and barged inside. Sergeant Francis O'Malley looked up from his desk, his eyes bulging. "Lieutenant! What in the—? You're alive!"

"It's *captain* now, Sergeant," Hammond rasped, jaw set in anger. "And I want to know if letters that I sent to Anita arrived in this office!"

With pallid face and weak voice, Sergeant O'Malley explained about Colonel Ballard's order that Hammond's letters to Anita should be diverted to the colonel.

From there Hammond went to the quarters where the Radcliffes and Art Ballard were now living, a modest apartment for married officers. Bill had been called away on routine duties, and Anita was alone. Greg stood at the door and told her what he had just learned from Sergeant O'Malley about the letters; then he said, "Anita, there is no way I can stay here and see you with Bill. You're his wife now. I'm going to the new commandant to ask for an immediate transfer."

Anita wiped the tears from her eyes and said, "Greg, darling, I still love you. You must believe that. I always will. I married Bill in the midst of all my grief, because I thought you were dead. I . . . don't know what to do."

Heavy of heart, Greg said, "You took vows, Anita.

You must stand by them. I will stay away from you all the time I have left here."

As he turned to leave, Anita called his name. When he looked back, she whispered, "I meant what I said. I will always love you."

"Same here," he replied, fighting his own tears as he turned to walk away.

At that moment Art Ballard came running up. "Greg!" he exclaimed. "I was outside the fort when you arrived. Boy, am I glad to see you!"

Hammond shook hands and then gave the youth a hug, explaining that he would be leaving the fort as soon as he could get transferred.

Art's face fell. "What happened?" he asked. "Why didn't we hear from you—"

Greg cut him off. "Anita will explain it to you. Right now I've got to go see the new commandant."

Chapter Fourteen

Captain Greg Hammond had to wait until afternoon to see Colonel William Branson, who had been meeting with Captains Payne and Cruz.

Branson spotted Hammond in the outer room after dismissing the officers and called him in. As they talked in private, the commandant was cordial, explaining that he had heard a lot of good things about Hammond, particularly from the sergeants and other enlisted men. "I'll admit I've heard some negative comments from Lieutenant Radcliffe," Branson confided, "but I'm aware of the situation between you two and figure his judgment is colored by personal feelings. I'm inclined to credit the opinions of the men."

"Thank you, sir," Hammond replied. "I appreciate that, and since you say you know how things are, it won't come as a surprise if I request an immediate transfer."

"No," Branson agreed. "In fact I'll admit your presence here leaves me with a dilemma: three captains—one too many. Obviously some mistake was made back in Washington; otherwise you'd never have been reassigned back here in the first place. It'll be straightened out, and you'll get your transfer, though I hate to lose a man like you. As a matter of fact, I've got a job for you right now."

"What's that, sir?"

"Your old friend Chago has gone on another killing spree. I hate to put a load on you so soon after your arrival, but after consulting with Captains Payne and Cruz, I've decided we need you to lead a unit and go after Chago. Our patrols have been scouring the area, but so far he has eluded us. You know his habits better than anyone else in this fort, so maybe you'll have better luck. Only one thing: Lieutenant Radcliffe will accompany you. He's more experienced than our other lieutenant, who in any case is out on patrol. Do you have any problems with that?"

Hammond was not happy about riding with his hated rival, but he saw no point in raising objections. A soldier did the job he was ordered to do, period. "None, sir," he replied evenly.

The party was to head out immediately, Colonel Branson added, for Chago had been seen in the area earlier in the day.

Hammond rose and left the office, and thirty minutes later the unit was assembling on the parade ground. As Sergeant Chuck Foster eased into his saddle, he told Greg Hammond how happy he was to see him alive. Hammond, swinging his leg over his own mount, was about to reply when his attention was drawn to Bill Radcliffe, who was kissing Anita not far away.

Anita stiffened when Radcliffe kissed her. Hammond could just overhear her husband speaking to her in a raised voice as he gripped her arms tightly. "You're *my* wife, Anita! Maybe Hammond was something to you in the past, but that's over and done with. He's not the only brave officer, you know! Just maybe *I* will be the one to get Chago!" He turned away from her and strode to his horse and mounted up.

The column of men in blue rode out, and as Hammond passed through the gate he glanced back at Anita. Even from this distance he could tell that her expression was one of pain and confusion, as if she were being torn apart inside. He knew that his love for her was stronger than it had ever been, and from all appearances she felt the same way. How could he leave Fort McDowell, knowing he would never see her again?

The daring and resourceful Chago had swung a war party of sixty Apaches within a few miles of the fort, hoping to find a small patrol he could wipe out. Having encountered none, he was leading his warriors back toward the Apache village when a scout came riding up from the direction of the fort.

The hard-faced leader signaled for his men to halt as the scout thundered to a stop in a cloud of dust. "Chago!" he said excitedly. "A band of soldier-coats has left the fort and is headed this way!"

"How many of them are coming?" asked Chago.

"I counted more than thirty."

A wicked look sprang into the Apache leader's dark eyes as he glanced at his braves. "We outnumber the white-eyes two to one. This day will not be a waste after all."

Chago sent the scout back out on the desert floor to keep an eye on the soldiers. The scout was to follow and confirm that they were still headed toward the Indians.

Chago meanwhile explored the area with his men, looking for a place from which to launch an ambush. When the scout returned, informing the leader that indeed the army patrol was coming straight toward them, Chago led his braves into a deep gulch that sided the path the soldiers were following. Leaving their horses in the gulch, they spread out along its edge and lay flat, guns ready. At their chief's signal they would rise up from their hiding places and blow the soldiers from their saddles.

Soon the Apaches could see the approaching column in the distance. A quarter hour brought them closer, so that the red men could hear the blowing of the army horses and the metallic clink of their military gear. Hunkering low, the Apaches waited, Chago keeping his head raised slightly, ready to give the signal when the entire unit had drawn abreast of them.

Suddenly Chago's body stiffened and his eyes widened. Seeing the face of the man he knew as Lieutenant Greg Hammond, he ran his fingertips over the ugly scar on his face. The violent death of his brother, Nachee, still vivid in his mind, Chago felt his heart quicken: The gods had delivered the hated white soldier to him!

For weeks the Apache leader had dreamed of killing Greg Hammond with his own hands, and simply to cut him down now with a hail of bullets would not do. Chago must meet him man-to-man and kill him in front of all the men in blue.

Quickly Chago sent the message along the line that Hammond was present; plans had changed, and at his signal the warriors were all to rise up, aiming their guns at the soldiers but not firing. Chago would challenge Hammond to meet him in a battle to the death.

The column of horse soldiers was relatively quiet as they moved through the hot afternoon sun. Hammond, riding beside Bill Radcliffe, ignored the sidelong glances of hatred that the lieutenant sent in his direction. Thinking of Anita, Greg sighed; when this was over, he knew, he would ride away for good, never to see her again.

Suddenly Hammond's attention was drawn to movement along the edge of the gulch at the right. A horde of Indians sprang up, each with a rifle pointed at the men in blue. The soldiers reacted instantly, drawing their own weapons, but Hammond saw the odds were against them, and he knew that if the Apaches had meant to do battle, they would already have been firing.

"Hold your fire, men!" shouted Hammond. "I think they want a powwow!"

It was then that Chago stepped forward. As the soldiers

kept their weapons trained on the Indians, anxiously
watching, Chago came to where the captain sat on his
horse. The chief leered maliciously and said, "Greg
Hammond! You have returned from fighting the Sioux. I
am surprised they not kill you like the dog you are!" He
glanced at Hammond's shoulder bars. "But I see you are
captain, now! Maybe you think you are even greater warrior.
But I tell you it is not so!"

Hammond's hatred for Chago had been smoldering
for weeks, and now it burst into flame. "Your men are not
firing at us, Chago," he said evenly. "What do you want?"

"*You!*" came the immediate reply. "I have long desired
to kill you with my own hands, and I am giving you a
challenge, Captain Greg Hammond: Fight with me man-to-
man! Accept the challenge, and you have my word that
when I have killed you, your men will not be harmed. But
refuse, and we will cut you down at once. What is your
answer?"

Hammond heard his men stir restlessly behind him as
they awaited his reply. He glanced over at Bill Radcliffe,
whose face wore a sinister smile; clearly the lieutenant
would have liked nothing better than to see Hammond cut
to shreds by Chago's knife.

Looking back at the chief, Captain Hammond knew
he had no choice. Not only did the Indians have the upper
hand; his own hatred for Chago gave him no alternative.
He would accept the challenge. He only hoped that the
warriors would honor Chago's promise, whatever the
outcome.

As Hammond laid aside his hat and stripped to the
waist, Chago ordered the soldiers to dismount. Confident
that they would not interfere—for to do so would be to
invite slaughter—he made no move to disarm them, but
he ordered his braves to keep their weapons trained on
them.

As the afternoon sun clearly illuminated the rippling
muscles in the bodies of both combatants, white men and

Indians alike looked on with tense interest. Chago threw Hammond a knife that was twin to his own, and Greg picked it up, wielding it to get the feel of it in his hand. Then the two enemies began to circle each other.

Chago suddenly charged, wailing like a banshee and swinging his deadly ten-inch blade at Hammond's midsection. The captain dodged nimbly and countered by striking the Apache on the ear with his left fist. Chago staggered but came right back, again jabbing with his knife. This time it bit into the flesh of Hammond's side, and the captain stumbled slightly. Chago cut him again and then danced away. Hammond winced with pain and wondered ruefully if the knife in Chago's hand had a life of its own. He could feel the blood flowing from both cuts, the second only an inch away from the first.

But now the pain and the danger of the moment shot fresh energy through the captain, and his hatred of Chago burned anew. This was the day he had lived for—but he forced himself to remain cool and calculating.

Chago was coming at him again, relishing the sight of his enemy's blood. This time Greg sidestepped the arc of the knife as it flashed past, and then he jumped in to counter with his own sharp weapon. The tip of Greg's knife found the flesh of Chago's left arm, cutting a gash about four inches long. Now Chago was bleeding.

Chago bellowed with rage at the sight of his own blood and then crouched low and lunged toward Hammond. Chago's knife missed Greg's shoulder, but the Apache's charge brought the two men so close that Greg could feel Chago's breath on his face. Hammond stepped back, slammed the Indian on the jaw with his left elbow, and cut a long, shallow furrow across his chest.

Reeling from his fresh wound, Chago nevertheless remained strong. He spat in the dust, cursed, and charged again. This time he fooled Hammond by suddenly dropping to the ground and extending his feet, thereby tripping his opponent. When the captain hit the ground, Chago dived for him, bringing the angry blade down toward his heart. Greg saw it coming and rolled away just in time.

The Apache rose to his feet, as did Hammond, and then charged again. Hammond was weakening, and Chago, seeing this, let out a whoop as he made a fierce thrust at the captain's chest with the deadly blade.

Greg barely managed to escape it. Chago, however, lost his balance for an instant, and Hammond was able to club him savagely with a balled-up left fist, sending him flat on his back.

Quick as a panther, Hammond was on top of the Indian, pressing the tip of the knife gently on the flesh just below his chin. Chago was helpless; one hostile move and the captain would plunge the blade deep into his throat.

Sweat poured from Hammond's face as he eyed his beaten enemy. All he had to do was finish him off by driving the blade deep.

As he paused, panting from his exertions, Hammond became aware that the Apaches were murmuring among themselves. He looked up to see the shock on their faces that their champion had been beaten, fairly and squarely. For many of them, Hammond knew, Chago had taken on godlike powers, and this defeat meant utter disillusionment.

The warriors looked expectant, awaiting Hammond's final blow. Looking down at Chago, Hammond knew what the chief was thinking: If he was not killed now, he would know only lifelong disgrace in the eyes of the entire tribe. Chago's pride was powerful, and he would rather die now than live.

Eyes wide, Chago pleaded, "Do it, white man! Kill me! Do not make me live in dishonor!"

Smiling, Hammond released the Indian and stood up.

"Please!" begged Chago again.

Without a word Greg Hammond spun around and walked toward his men, a smile of victory pressed on his lips.

Chago raised up on one elbow, his face gaunt with

rage and shame. "Captain Greg Hammond!" he screamed. "Kill me! I command it! Kill me!"

As Hammond drew closer to his men he glanced back at the Apaches, who were regarding their leader with scorn.

Then Hammond heard Lieutenant Radcliffe calling to him. "You couldn't finish him, Hammond, could you? You're still the Indian-lover you always were! What will Anita think when she finds out that *I* had to do the job for you!"

The lieutenant abruptly pulled his service revolver and cocked it as he dashed toward Chago. Hammond saw what he was doing and shouted for him to stop, but it was too late. The headstrong lieutenant fired twice into Chago's chest, and the Indian slumped down. Then a dozen Apache rifles boomed, riddling the lieutenant with bullets, and Radcliffe fell.

Hammond, knowing instinctively that his men would want to open fire at once, shouted at them to hold their fire. He knew that all his men would die if a general gunfight broke out.

Hearing the captain's order, the Apache warrior who was second in command raised his hand for his braves to do likewise. Then he stepped close and looked hard at Hammond. "You are wise not to shoot, Captain, for we outnumber you. And I tell you this: What you did to Chago was wicked. You have shamed us by failing to kill him honorably on the field of combat. You have disgraced him by letting him be cut down by gunfire, like a dog. If you want your men to live, you must answer to this yourself before our leader, Amanzus. Come with us, and we will honor Chago's promise that your men shall go unharmed. If you do not come, you will all die."

Greg Hammond heard his men stirring, no doubt thinking what he was thinking: Once he was in the Indian camp, there was no telling what would happen to him. But his men had no chance of survival if they did battle with the Apache horde that surrounded them. Once again Greg Hammond had no choice. As he put on his shirt, he said to Sergeant Foster, "Take the men and go."

"But, sir!" protested Foster. "We can't just—"

"Now!" commanded the captain. "That's an order, Sergeant!"

The soldiers picked up Bill Radcliffe's body and draped it over his horse. As they mounted up and rode away Hammond spotted some of them looking regretfully over their shoulders as he himself climbed into his saddle. The angry Apaches picked up the body of Chago, and one of the Indians took the reins of his horse. Hammond was their captive.

When the men arrived at Fort McDowell that afternoon, nearly every soldier in the fort gathered on the parade ground to hear what had happened. Colonel Branson was standing near Sergeant Foster, who described the incident. The men rejoiced to know that Chago was dead, but all were profoundly troubled by Greg Hammond's capture.

Anita Radcliffe came onto the parade ground as the sergeant was completing his account, and he went to her and broke the news of Radcliffe's death. As the colonel also tried to comfort her, she shed tears for her husband because of the violent way he had died, but her deeper concern was for the man she loved.

Anita turned to the commandant. "Colonel," she asked, "what are we going to do about Greg?"

Looking somber, Branson replied dully, "I'm afraid there's nothing we *can* do, at least not until we get reinforcements. The Apaches have so many more warriors than we have soldiers that I would be asking all of these men to commit suicide to attempt a rescue."

Anita started to protest bitterly but then stopped herself. As a commandant's daughter she recalled similar difficult decisions her father had had to make while he was alive. Reluctantly she acknowledged that Branson's reaction was the only proper one under the circumstances.

As the crowd of soldiers dispersed, she remained on the parade ground, pacing up and down by herself. She decided that nothing was as important at that moment as Greg Hammond's life. She quickly made up her mind that she would sneak out of the fort and ride to the Apache village. She knew the way—her father had taken her there once, shortly after signing his pact with Amanzus. There was one thing she could do that might save Greg's life. . . .

Within minutes the determined young woman had taken a horse and slipped unnoticed through a side gate. She rode like the wind toward the lowering sun, weeping and praying that God would let Greg live until she arrived.

The miles flew by, Anita scarcely aware of her surroundings. Drawing near the village, she slowed her horse to a walk as she moved past Apache huts, looking for Amanzus and for Greg. All she saw were strangers, the curious faces of men, women, and children who looked up and stared at her. Not speaking the Apache language, she had difficulty making herself understood by the suspicious Indians, but finally, by repeating the name Amanzus, she found one woman who directed her to a hut at the far end of the village.

Pressing her horse in that direction, she prepared herself for what was about to come. As she approached Amanzus's hut, which was larger than the others, her eyes widened when she saw two men standing in front of it, engaged in conversation. One of them was Simino . . . and the other was Greg Hammond!

Both men turned toward her as she rode up. Her name broke on Greg's lips, and he dashed to her; as she dismounted, he folded her in his arms. Anita burst into tears and clung to him.

While Simino looked on, Hammond held her at arm's length and said, "Anita, why are you here?"

Sucking in a quivering breath, she replied, "Oh,

darling, I . . . came to offer myself as a ransom, a prisoner, if Chief Amanzus would let you live."

Hammond embraced her again, and while he held her, he whispered, "You are a woman beyond belief! I don't know what to say. Everything's all right, though. Amanzus has let me go."

Anita's weeping increased in volume.

"You remember when I kept Bill from killing Simino?"

Anita nodded, sobbing with joy.

"Well, since I had saved Simino's life, his father and he have now saved mine."

Overcome with happiness, Anita left Hammond and embraced Simino. The Apache was shocked as she squeezed his neck and thanked him for what he had just done. When she released him, she saw a slight glistening in his dark eyes.

Hammond and Simino shook hands, and then the handsome captain looked down at Anita and said, "I'm sorry about Bill."

Anita raised her eyes to his and said, "I'm sorry that he died such a violent death, but I guess it had to be. He seemed bent on something like that when he left the fort."

Greg nodded silently.

At this moment the flap of the hut opened and Anita saw the old Apache chief whom she knew to be Amanzus. Simino explained why she had come, and the chief came over to her. Laying a gentle hand on her shoulder, he gazed into her eyes, a look of admiration on his face.

"We think as much of Captain Greg Hammond as you do," the old man said. "Amanzus thinks Greg Hammond is lucky to know such a one as you."

Greg shook hands with both Amanzus and Simino, and turning to Anita, he said, "We'd better be going." He started toward his bay, tethered nearby.

Grasping his arm and pulling him around, Anita said, "Wait. I have to know something right now."

"Yes?"

"With Bill . . . gone, I am no longer bound by my vows. Do . . . do you still want me?"

Heaving a long sigh, Greg took her in his arms. "More than ever!"

As Greg and Anita stepped up to the horses, he asked, "How about riding on mine with me?"

"I'd love it," she smiled.

He put his hands on her slender waist and then said, "I'm going to take the transfer when it comes through. You can go with me, and we'll marry wherever the army puts me. Art can come along if he wants."

Smiling, the beautiful redhead saluted and said, "Yes, sir, Captain Hammond!"

Their lips blended in another kiss; then Greg Hammond lifted Anita into his saddle and swung up behind her. As they rode out, the other horse trailing behind, they looked back to see Amanzus and Simino still standing there, each raising a hand in farewell. Anita and Greg waved, and then the young couple turned and pressed forward, riding through the golds and purples of the setting sun, across the broad desert toward Fort McDowell.

Author's Note

At the end of the Civil War, the United States Army was assigned the onerous task of "pacifying" the Indians of numerous hostile and rebellious tribes spread across more than a million square miles of territory, from Kansas to the Sierra Nevada, from Dakota Territory to west Texas, as white settlers—encouraged in part by the Homestead Act of 1862—moved onto the land of America's last great frontier.

The army, reduced in size by acts of Congress to some 28,000 men by 1876, had the responsibility of manning several dozen far-flung forts, of which Fort McDowell was one. Established as Camp McDowell in 1865, the fort existed until 1891 in the location described in *Apache Junction*.

For purposes of the story Apache Junction has been placed in its present-day location. Some liberty has been taken in supposing that a settlement existed in this spot as early as 1876, but towns like the one in the story were commonplace along stagecoach routes throughout Arizona and the West. The two stage lines mentioned—the California & Arizona Stage Company and the Southern Pacific Mail Line—both operated in 1876, and their intersection in Florence, then a town the size of Phoenix, was mentioned in a guidebook to Arizona published in 1877.